Ruby

Annabelle Starr

EGMONT

Special thanks to:

Kirsty Neale, St John's Walworth Church of England School
and Belmont Primary School

EGMONT

We bring stories to life

Published in Great Britain 2007
by Egmont UK Limited
239 Kensington High Street, London W8 6SA

Text & illustration © 2007 Egmont UK Ltd
Text by Kirsty Neale
Illustrations by Helen Turner

ISBN 978 1 4052 3250 0

1 3 5 7 9 10 8 6 4 2

A CIP catalogue record for this title is available
from the British Library

Typeset by Avon DataSet Ltd, Bidford on Avon, Warwickshire
Printed and bound in Great Britain by the CPI Group

Meet the
Megastar Mysteries Team!

Hi, this is me, **Rosie Parker** (otherwise known as Nosy Parker), and these are my best mates . . .

. . . **Soph** (Sophie) **McCoy** – she's a real fashionista sista – and . . .

. . . **Abs** (Abigail) **Flynn**, who's officially une grande genius.

Here's my mum, **Liz Parker**. Much to my embarrassment, her fashion and music taste is well and truly stuck in the 1980s (but despite all that I still love her dearly) . . .

. . . and my nan, **Pam Parker**, the murder-mystery freak I mentioned on the cover. Sometimes, just sometimes, her crackpot ideas do come in handy.

Consider yourself introduced!

ROSIE'S MINI MEGASTAR PHRASEBOOK

Want to speak our lingo, but don't know your soeurs from your signorinas? No problemo! Just use my comprehensive guide . . .

-a-rama	add this ending to a word to indicate a large quantity: e.g. 'The after-show party was celeb-a-rama'
amigo	Spanish for 'friend'
au contraire, mon frère	French for 'on the contrary, my brother'
au revoir	French for 'goodbye'
barf/barfy/barfissimo	sick/sick-making/very sick-making indeed
bien sûr, ma soeur	French for 'of course, my sister'
bon	French for 'good'
bonjour	French for 'hello'
celeb	short for 'celebrity'
convo	short for 'conversation'
cringe-fest	a highly embarrassing situation
Cringeville	a place we all visit from time to time when something truly embarrassing happens to us
cringeworthy	an embarrassing person, place or thing might be described as this
daggy	Australian for 'unfashionable' or unstylish'
doco	short for 'documentary'
exactamundo	not a real foreign word, but a great way to express your agreement with someone
exactement	French for 'exactly'

excusez moi	French for 'excuse me'
fashionista	'a keen follower of fashion' – can be teamed with 'sista' for added rhyming fun
glam	short for 'glamorous'
gorge/gorgey	short for 'gorgeous': e.g. 'the lead singer of that band is gorge/gorgey'
hilarioso	not a foreign word at all, just a great way to liven up 'hilarious'
hola, señora	Spanish for 'hello, missus'
hottie	no, this is *not* short for hot water bottle – it's how you might describe an attractive-looking boy to your friends
-issimo	try adding this ending to English adjectives for extra emphasis: e.g. coolissimo, crazissimo – très funissimo, non?
je ne sais pas	French for 'I don't know'
je voudrais un beau garçon, s'il vous plaît	French for 'I would like an attractive boy, please'
journos	short for 'journalists'
les Français	French for, erm, 'the French'
Loserville	this is where losers live, particularly evil school bully Amanda Hawkins
mais	French for 'but'
marvelloso	not technically a foreign word, just a more exotic version of 'marvellous'
massivo	Italian for 'massive'
mon amie/mes amis	French for 'my friend'/'my friends'
muchos	Spanish for 'many'

non	French for 'no'
nous avons deux garçons ici	French for 'we have two boys here'
no way, José!	'that's never going to happen!'
oui	French for 'yes'
quelle horreur!	French for 'what horror!'
quelle surprise!	French for 'what a surprise!'
sacré bleu	French for 'gosh' or even 'blimey'
stupido	this is the Italian for 'stupid' – stupid!
-tastic	add this ending to any word to indicate a lot of something: e.g. 'Abs is braintastic'
très	French for 'very'
swoonsome	decidedly attractive
si, si, signor/signorina	Italian for 'yes, yes, mister/miss'
terriblement	French for 'terribly'
une grande	French for 'a big' – add the word 'genius' and you have the perfect description of Abs
Vogue	it's only the world's most influential fashion magazine, darling!
voilà	French for 'there it is'
what's the story, Rory?	'what's going on?'
what's the plan, Stan?	'which course of action do you think we should take?'
what the crusty old grandads?	'what on earth?'
zut alors!	French for 'darn it!'

Hi Megastar reader!

My name's Annabelle Starr*. I'm a fashion stylist – just like Soph's Aunt Penny – which means it's my job to help celebrities look their best at all times.

Over the years, I've worked with all sorts of big names, some of whom also have seriously big egos! Take the time I flew all the way to Japan to style a shoot for a girl band. One of the members refused to wear the designer number I'd picked out for her and insisted on sporting a dress her mum had run up from some revolting old curtains instead. The only way I could get her to take it off was to persuade her it didn't match her pet Pekinese's outfit!

Anyway, when I first started out, I never dreamt I'd write a series of books based around my crazy celebrity experiences, but that's just what I've done with Megastar Mysteries. Rosie, Soph and Abs have just the sort of adventures I wish my friends and I could have got up to when we were teenagers!

I really hope you enjoy reading the books as much as I enjoyed writing them!

Love **Annabelle**

* I'll let you in to a little secret: this isn't my real name, but in this business you can never be too careful!

Chapter One

When it comes to buying birthday presents, I am officially a genius. I've known my best friend, Abs, practically forever, but every year I come up with an even cooler present than the last one. I have this formula where you write down the person's name, the stuff they like and dislike and then the present they'd want if you were mega-rich and could buy anything. Then you add an extra bit at the bottom for a version of the present you can afford.

So, for Abs's birthday, it went like this:

Person: Abs
Likes: Me and Soph (i.e. best friends),
music, shopping, make-up, TV, books,
animals and chocolate
Dislikes: Amanda Hawkins, boring films,
drama lessons, cabbage and Amanda Hawkins
**Present she would ask for if I was
mega-rich:** A trip to New York
Similar thing that I can afford:
A chocolate skyscraper (not life-size, obviously)
and a new lipgloss called American Sweetheart

Brilliant, eh?

Unfortunately for Abs, not everyone is quite up
to my incredibly high standards on the present-
buying front. Like her parents. Did they buy her
the new mobile she's been dropping massivo hints
about for the last month? Or a CD player to
replace the one that hasn't worked since her little
sis tried to feed it a biscuit? No, they did not.

'So what did you get?' me and Soph asked Abs
when she arrived at school on the morning of her

birthday. Checking the present-haul is always top priority on birthdays.

Abs pulled a glossy leaflet out of her bag and passed it to us. 'A day in a recording studio,' she said, sounding not-at-all-thrilled.

'You lie!' said Soph.

'I wish,' said Abs. 'Why couldn't they just have got me the phone?'

'This is so cool,' I said, reading the leaflet. 'You record any songs you want, then they turn it into a professional CD and even take your photo to go on the CD cover.'

'It'll be seriously cringe-issimo,' Abs argued. 'I can't stand there and sing in front of some record producer. I don't even sing in the shower in case Mum and Dad hear.'

'But you've got a really good voice,' said Soph, who sounds like a sackful of cheesed-off cats when she sings.

'What about when we were Mirage's backing singers?' I chipped in. The three of us had solved this huge mystery for Mirage Mullins just after her first single got to number one, and she'd thanked us by letting us be her backing singers. 'We were on stage in front of hundreds of people.'

'That was different,' said Abs. 'We were miming, remember?'

I flipped through the leaflet again, then handed it back to Abs, pointing at the second page.

'It says "Solo singers and groups welcome",' I said. 'Me and Soph could come with you.'

Abs hesitated. 'Really?'

'Course. I mean, if it makes you feel better . . .'

'Totally,' said Abs, looking much happier. 'It would be a million times easier with all of us there.'

'What are friends for?' said Soph.

Me and Abs grinned.

'In your case, Soph,' I said, 'to make everyone else sound better than Britney.'

* * *

Abs's day in the studio was booked for the following Saturday, and by the time we got there we were all majorly excited. Soph had spent the whole week turning another of her weird charity-shop finds into a seriously cool outfit for the occasion, while me and Abs had sent about a million texts trying to decide what we were going to sing. We'd narrowed it down to Fusion's latest single (in honour of the fact I met them last year and got to snog très gorge lead singer, Maff), one of the songs we'd sung on stage with Mirage last year (because it's a mega-cool memory) and Abs's favourite Girls Aloud hit (because they rock). My mum was a bit sulky when she found out we hadn't gone with any of her suggestions. As I pointed out, this is the twenty-first century and unless they had a parent in a Bananarama tribute band like I have, the producers would probably never have heard of half the eighties stuff she'd suggested.

Icon Studios was pretty cool. Considering we were in Fleetwich – the only place in the world that makes our dullsville hometown, Borehurst, look like a hive of thrill-a-minute activity – I'd half expected it to be yet another grey tower block, but it totally wasn't. Abs's mum had driven us in through a narrow passage between a bank and a shop selling fishing equipment (I told you it was exciting), into a sort of hidden courtyard. The studio building stretched around three sides in a squared-off U-shape, and was a strange mixture of old brick and shiny new glass. It looked seriously smart and showbizzy.

'I could so imagine being a huge star, turning up here in my chauffeur-driven limo,' whispered Soph as we walked through the glass doors, which had slid open silently to let us through.

'D'you know where we're meant to go?' I asked Abs, looking round at the super-sleek reception area. The walls were lined with CD-cover artwork in silver frames and there was a curving metal and wooden staircase in the corner.

'Reception,' said Abs, walking over to the huge, white reception desk.

A few seconds later, she came back.

'The receptionist says to take a seat and our producer will be out in a minute.'

The three of us perched on a row of cool orange chairs set against one wall. The receptionist gave us a faint smile. There was a corridor opposite us with a sign that said 'Studios A-E'. As I watched, a tall, brown-haired dream-god walked along it towards us.

'Abigail?' he said.

'Hi,' I said swoonily.

'Er, *I'm* Abigail,' said Abs, flashing me one of her famous death-stares.

'Will,' said Mr Dreamy, shaking her hand. 'I'm your producer.'

'These are my friends,' said Abs. 'Soph,' – Soph shook his hand – 'and –'

'Posie,' I interrupted, sticking my hand out. 'Posie Rarker. I mean Rarky Poser.'

'Rosie Parker,' Abs corrected me.

'It's good to meet you all,' said Will.

He gave me a bit of a funny look, and I realised I was still shaking his hand. I let go, and smiled at him in what I hoped was a reassuringly I-am-not-a-mad-person way.

'Shall we make a start?' he said, backing away from me quite quickly.

Rosie Parker's really useful guide to recording your own CD:

1. Listen very carefully when your dream-god producer is giving you a tour of the studio. The room where you sing into the microphone is called the live room, not the padded room. Padded rooms are only found in loony bins.

2. The producer's bit of the studio is the control room. The giant desk with all the knobs and buttons and slidey bits is the mixing desk. If you ask 'what does that one do?' about every single one, you will end up with less than half an hour to actually sing your songs and will still not really understand the knobs.

3. Leaning in to the microphone and saying 'one-two, one-two, testing, one-two' will not make anyone except you laugh.

4. Just because you cannot hear your producer through the glass window in the live room, it is not safe to assume he cannot hear you. Going on about how gorgey he is, then watching him look horrified is not a good way of testing who can hear who.

5. When your producer suggests you should warm up, he means warm up your voice by singing through your songs a few times, not warm up your body by doing star jumps and jogging on the spot.

6. Trying to flip your hair (as recommended in *Star Secrets'* Twenty Top Flirting Tips feature) when you're wearing headphones is not a) safe, b) a good idea, or c) at all attractive.

7. Saying 'cheese' when having your photo taken for the CD cover will make your smile look like Wallace from *Wallace and Gromit*. (Do I need to explain why this is not a good thing?)

8. Getting really into the song and deciding to try some Christina-Aguilera-style improvisation

will just make the producer think you've forgotten the tune. Don't add in extra 'oh yeah' or 'ooh, baby' bits, either.

'That's great,' said Will as we finished the last song.

'Are you sure?' said Abs. 'Soph was squawking in the last chorus.'

'Oi!' said Soph indignantly. 'I do *not* squawk. The microphone must have been out of tune.'

Will grinned. 'Take off your headphones, come in here and let's have a listen.'

He pulled three extra chairs up to his mixing desk for us.

'This,' he said, 'is the good bit.'

'I thought our singing was the good bit,' I said.

'Yeees,' he said slowly, looking a bit shiftily in Soph's direction. 'But this . . . helps things along – smoothes everything out. Listen.'

He pressed a couple of buttons and the room was suddenly filled with the sound of our voices over the backing track. Me and Abs gaped at each other, horrified. It sounded très terrible.

'Cool,' said Soph, nodding her head along to the music.

She really is completely tone deaf.

Will turned it down a bit.

'If I do this,' he said, fiddling on the desk again, 'I can separate your voices out. So that's just Rosie.'

We listened for a minute. Sometimes I wonder if it's fair to deprive the world of my marvelloso voice by being a mega-successful journalist instead of a singer.

'This is Abs,' said Will, switching to a different voice and forgetting to comment on my brilliantness. 'And then Soph.'

Which was where it sort of fell apart.

'Is there a dog loose in the studio?' said Abs, and Soph kicked her in the shins.

Will laughed and tapped away at the computer which was sitting next to his mixing desk, then pressed play again.

'Who's that?' I said, as a fourth voice filled the studio.

'Soph,' he said.

'No way!' me and Abs said together.

'Oh, yeah,' said Soph. 'I totally rock.'

'How did you do that?' I asked.

'It's called pitch correction,' Will explained. 'It turns all Soph's wrong notes into the right ones so she's in tune.'

'We should get one of those for the music room at school,' said Abs, as Will carried on working.

'Maybe we could have one fitted in Soph's hairbrush,' I suggested.

* * *

Twenty minutes later, Will had finished pitch-correcting Soph, and worked a few more producery tricks on our songs. We now sounded like a serious threat to the Sugababes. We'd chosen a photo for the CD cover from the ones he'd taken earlier, and even though I was trying really hard to get some gossip from Will about celebs he had worked with, we'd just about run out of excuses to hang around.

'It's my mum,' said Abs, opening the text message she'd just received. 'She's waiting outside.'

We all said thanks to Will, and he reminded us to order extra copies of our CD in reception before we left.

'You did a great job,' he said.

'I still can't believe that was my voice,' said Soph as we walked back along the studio corridor.

'Me neither,' said Abs.

'Will thought we were great,' I said dreamily.

'Maybe we should start a group,' said Abs.

'Oui, oui!' Soph flung her arms out towards an invisible audience. 'Ladies and gentlemen, live from boring Borehurst, please welcome Soph and the Sophettes!'

'Hey,' I said, 'since when was this *your* band?'

'Yeah,' said Abs, with an evil glint in her eye. 'How about "Please welcome the Rarky Posers" instead?'

I felt my face turn redder than a monkey's bum. 'I couldn't help it. It's not my fault he's —'

But before I could say anything else, we crashed

into this complete stranger who'd appeared out of nowhere. As soon as we'd untangled ourselves, I realised she'd just come out of one of the other studios along the corridor.

'I'm really sorry,' I said to the stranger, who didn't look that much older than us. 'We totally weren't watching where we were going.'

'Are you OK?' Soph asked.

'I'm fine,' she grinned.

'We should've been paying more attention,' said Abs. 'We were just messing about.'

'I heard,' said the girl, still smiling. 'So who's Rarky Poser?'

I blushed again. 'That'd be me,' I said. 'Rosie Parker.'

'Nice to meet you, Rosie Parker,' she said. 'I'm Ruby Munday.'

I stared at her, wondering why that name sounded familiar.

'Awful, isn't it?' she nodded. 'I probably should have changed it.'

'How d'you mean, awful?' said Soph.

'Ruby Munday. Like the song, "Ruby Tuesday",' said Ruby.

'The Rolling Stones!' said Abs. 'My dad loves them.'

Ruby nodded. 'My parents have been fans for years. When I was born, they thought it would be really hilarious to call me Ruby, and I've been stuck with people making jokes about it ever since.'

'Sounds like they'd get on with my mum,' I said grimly. 'I mean, who in their right mind calls their daughter Rosie when their surname is Parker?'

Ruby laughed. 'So are you three in a band, then?' she said.

'I wish,' said Soph.

Abs explained about her birthday present. 'We've had a brilliant time. This place is awesome.'

'It's OK, isn't it?' Ruby agreed. 'I'm here loads at the moment.'

'Are you in a band?' asked Abs.

'No,' said Ruby. 'I'm recording an album, but it's just me. I mean, I've got backing musicians, but

I write my own songs, and sing, and play a bit of guitar and stuff.'

'That must be so cool,' I said.

She frowned, and I noticed how tired she looked. 'I love it, but it's my first album and it has to be perfect, you know? There's a lot of pressure to get it just right, or I might not get the chance to make another.' She smiled again. 'It *is* a pretty cool job most of the time, though.'

The studio door opened and a man wearing a black hat stuck his head out. 'We need you back in fifteen, Rubes,' he told her.

Ruby pointed at another door a little way along the corridor. According to a paper sign taped to it, it was the chill-out lounge. 'I really need to go and get some coffee,' she said. 'And, you know . . .'

'Chill out?' said Abs.

'Exactly,' Ruby giggled. 'It was really good to meet you all.'

'You, too,' I said.

Abs looked at her watch. 'My mum is going to kill us,' she said.

Chapter Two

'Wait,' said Soph as we hurried back through reception. 'We've got to order the extra CDs.'

Abs looked out anxiously at her mum who was waiting in the courtyard in her car.

'Where's that copy of our CD that Will gave you?' I said, having a mini-brainwave.

'In my bag,' said Abs. 'Why?'

'Give it to your mum to play in the car, and tell her we'll be another ten minutes. You know what parents are like – she'll be all proud and distracted, and forget how long she's been waiting.'

'Good thinking, Batgirl,' said Abs, heading out through the sliding doors.

'Hi,' I said, walking up to the receptionist. 'We need to order some extra CDs.'

'Sure,' said the receptionist. 'It was Studio A, wasn't it? Booked in the name of Flynn.'

I nodded.

'No problem,' she said. 'How many do you need?'

'Seven for me,' I said. 'Soph?'

'Well,' said Soph, 'there's Aunt Penny, and Auntie Sheila and Uncle Herman; Dad wants one for his boss, plus there's Mrs Davidson next door . . .'

She carried on counting people off on her fingers while the receptionist stared at her.

'So that's fourteen for me,' said Soph. 'And didn't your mum say we should get a few spares to send out to record companies?' she added.

Oh joy. Another of my mum's loonissimo schemes revealed to a total stranger.

'She's always getting these weird ideas,' I told the receptionist. I meant my mum, not Soph, although some days it's a close call. The receptionist gave me a sympathetic look.

'Let's make it thirty altogether,' said Soph.

'And what about your friend?' the receptionist asked.

Me and Soph looked out into the courtyard. Abs was leaning through the car window, talking to her mum.

'I'm not sure,' I said.

'I'll go and ask her,' said Soph, and she dashed off.

'So, how did your session go?' the receptionist asked. 'Will's great, isn't he?'

'Totally,' I said. 'And he made us sound amazing, even Soph – she's got a voice that makes you want to chop your own ears off.'

'Have you done any singing before?' said the receptionist.

I told her about Mirage and the backing-singers thing.

'I love Mirage!' she said.

'Me, too,' I said. 'I'm Rosie, by the way.'

'Nadia,' she smiled. 'It's so nice to have someone in here who's into the same kind of music as me. Most of the people we get like total rubbish. You know, the kind of stuff your dad thinks is cool.'

'It can't be any worse than my mum's obsession with the eighties,' I said. 'But what about that girl – Ruby? She said she was here all the time and she's not into old stuff.'

Nadia got this really excited look on her face and leaned forwards over her desk in a way that totally said 'gossip ahoy'.

'You know Ruby?'

'We bumped into her in the corridor a few minutes ago,' I said. 'She seemed really cool, but . . .'

'But what?' said Nadia eagerly.

'I'm sure I know her name from somewhere,' I frowned. 'I just can't remember where.'

'She's Ruby Munday!' said Nadia. 'The child star. She was an actress – *Wish Upon A Star*? *My New Mum*? *Double Trouble*?'

Something sort of clicked in my brain. I'd seen *Double Trouble* once, a long time ago.

'Didn't she play twins or something?' I said, trying to remember.

'Yes!' said Nadia. 'It was all done with trick photography. She had to film nearly every scene twice, just changing her hair and clothes between takes. They had a double for when you just saw her back, you know, talking to her twin – herself, I mean – but apart from that, it was all Ruby.'

'What's the story, Rory?' said Soph as she walked back into reception with Abs.

'Nadia was telling me about Ruby,' I said. 'She used to be an actress.'

'Ooh, did you?' said Soph, looking excitedly at Nadia. 'What have you been in?'

'No, *Ruby* was an actress, Soph,' I said.

'Of course!' said Abs, suddenly. 'That's why I recognised her name. She was in that film about the twins.'

'But if she's an actress, why is she here recording an album?' said Soph.

'Yeah,' I said, turning back to Nadia. 'I was wondering about that too.'

'It's her big comeback,' said Nadia. 'She hasn't made a film for about ten years, but now she's back doing music instead. It was always her first love anyway. Well, that and animals.'

'How di–' I started to say, but Nadia was on a bit of a Ruby-roll now.

'That was why she had such a good time making *Puppies For Sale* – her love of animals. They actually let her take one of the puppies home when they'd finished filming. She called it Toffee, but her mum and dad made her give it away after it ate all these really expensive fish out of the pond in their back garden.'

We were all gaping at Nadia. It seemed like there was nothing she didn't know about Ruby. Super-fan or what?

'So after that,' Nadia went on, 'she decided to stick to music. She said it was less heartbreaking. Her favourite thing was singing – they actually let her do that in *Little Miss Lovely* – but she had guitar lessons and a piano teacher, too.'

'Wow,' I said, butting in when Nadia stopped to take a breath. 'That's –'

A car horn hooted from out in the courtyard.

'That's my mum,' Abs said hastily. 'We'd better go.'

'The CDs!' said Soph. 'I nearly forgot.'

'So did I,' said Nadia. 'How many d'you want?'

'Forty,' said Soph. 'That's for all of us.'

'No problem,' said Nadia, tapping her keyboard. 'You can pick them up on Tuesday.'

'See you then,' I said.

'See you,' Nadia said, giving us a beaming smile.

'Can you believe we've just recorded a CD next door to an actual movie star?' said Soph, as we headed for the door.

'We are sooo cool,' said Abs. 'I wonder who else knows she's planning a comeback.'

'I bet Amanda Hawkins doesn't,' I said.

Amanda is my least favourite person in the entire world.

'So when are we going to tell her?' said Soph.

'And just how much will we enjoy rubbing her annoyingly perfect nose in it?' added Abs.

The glass entrance doors slid silently open to let us out and I turned to wave goodbye to Nadia. In the few seconds it had taken us to reach the door, her face had gone from friendly and smiling to frowning and totally narky. I paused mid-wave, but as soon as she realised I was looking at her, Nadia switched her smile on again and waved back at me.

'Oi – Rarky Poser,' said Abs, tugging at my arm, 'get a move on!'

'Rarky what?' said her mum through the car window.

Chapter Three

The best thing about Abs's house is how normal it is. You'd never find her mum wearing legwarmers or practising dance routines for yet another Bananarama tribute-band gig, mostly because her mum isn't in a Bananarama tribute band. Mrs Flynn does normal mum stuff, like shopping, and taking Abs's little sister, Megan, to the park, and making dinner without setting off the smoke alarm. Mr F is nicely normal, too. He works in an office and at the weekend he does things in his shed or puts up shelves. When I mentioned the lovely normalness to Abs after our day in the recording studio, she gave me this look like I'd grown an extra nose. We were hanging out in her room, waiting for pizzas to be delivered as an end-of-Abs's-birthday-present treat.

'You think my house is normal?' she said incredulously.

'Yes,' I said. 'Like when we got back, and your mum didn't try to force-feed us tea and custard creams.'

This is my nan's second-favourite pastime after murder mysteries.

'And,' I continued, 'your dad's dressed like he actually knows what year it is. It's just . . . normal.'

Abs switched her computer on so we could look up Ruby Munday on the Internet.

'The reason Mum let us come up here,' she said, 'is because Megan was having a snot explosion in the middle of the kitchen and she needed to clear it up. And those things my dad was wearing are his DIY clothes. They're so ancient, they've actually come back into fashion. Believe me,' she added, 'you do *not* want to see what he wears when we go out.'

'It couldn't be worse than legwarmers and a ra-ra skirt,' I said.

'Ew,' groaned Abs, 'can you imagine my dad's hairy legs in a ra-ra skirt?'

'Ooh la la!' squealed Soph, and we all went a bit bonkers laughing.

'OK,' said Abs, trying to be sensible after a few minutes. 'Ruby Munday.'

'Yes,' I said, dragging up a spare chair to sit next to her at the desk.

She typed Ruby's name into the search engine, then clicked on the first result, which was a really short entry on MovieStarInfo.com:

NAME: Ruby Enid Munday

AGE: 19

FILMS: *Wish Upon A Star, My New Mum, Scoot!, Double Trouble, The Treasure Trap, Little Miss Lovely, Puppies For Sale, SpaceKids 2050, Jenny Jewel, Don't Tell Dad*

OTHER: Child star, Munday, made her last film, aged just 10, before disappearing from the public eye completely.

'Enid?' giggled Soph.

'It's probably after her great aunt or something,' said Abs, whose middle name is Florence.

'That thing about disappearing fits in with what Nadia told us,' I said, ignoring them. 'It doesn't say why, though. See if you can find anything else.'

Abs clicked on the next link. It was another movie site, but this one had comments from film fans. There were loads of messages saying things like 'Where is Ruby now?', 'Anyone heard what Ruby's been up to since she stopped making films?' and 'I reckon Ruby couldn't handle the fame. She is probably living in the Outer Hebrides'. And that was one of the least freaky suggestions.

'Look at this one,' I said. '"Ruby was a boy dressed up as a girl. When the papers found out, he had to retire from films."'

'This person can't even spell properly,' said Abs, scrolling down the page. (She is quite strict about things like that.) '"Ruby was a rite good actriss and she wood still of been a star if it weren't for the coppers who did her for croolty to fish."'

"Ruby Munday works in my local branch of Bigger Burgers",' read Soph.

By now, my mystery radar was well and truly whirling. If anyone knew what had happened to Ruby, there wouldn't be all these stupid theories floating around. We tried a few more sites and eventually found a newspaper article from about a year after Ruby made her last film:

GOODBYE, RUBY MUNDAY
Has the curse of the child star struck again?

More than a year after the release of her last film, Don't Tell Dad, Ruby Munday's agent today confirmed the child star would not be making any more movies in the near future. Her contract with DreamFilms expired six months ago and, despite numerous attempts to track Ruby down, she has not been seen in public since the premiere of Don't Tell Dad last November. Her agent refused to give any information on Ruby's decision to quit the movie business, or to say where she is currently living. Could it be that, like many unfortunate child stars of the past, Miss Munday has simply burned out? Making ten films in the five years since she started in the business, it would not be surprising if her health had suffered.

Several film critics have also suggested that Ruby, now aged ten, was dropped by DreamFilms because they felt she was no longer cute enough for their highly successful children's films. Whatever lies behind Ruby Munday's sudden disappearance from the limelight, the real-life story of this child star will continue to intrigue movie audiences for some time yet.

'I knew it!'

'Knew what?' said Soph.

'That there was something mysterious about it,' I said.

'Mmm,' said Abs doubtfully. 'Except, there isn't really, is there? It's just newspaper talk. They're always making normal things sound way more exciting and mysterious than they actually are.'

'And that's from, like, forever ago,' Soph pointed out. 'Years and years. Keep looking, Abs.'

But even though we spent another twenty minutes searching, the same thing came up again and again – Ruby made her last film nearly ten years ago, and then disappeared without an explanation.

The doorbell rang and Abs's mum shouted that the pizzas had arrived. Abs turned her computer off.

'It's probably something totally simplissimo,' she said. 'Ruby got bored with acting or something.'

'Like me,' said Soph. 'When I was ten, I went right off horse riding. I stopped going and I've never been back since.'

'Yeah, but you didn't get paid thousands of pounds every time you went out for a canter,' I said.

'Think about it,' said Abs. 'We met Ruby today, and she was really cool. Happy, fun, seriously gorgeous, doing her own thing –'

'Amazing shoes,' chipped in Soph.

'She was as normal as you and me,' said Abs. 'Well, me anyway.'

I threw a pillow at her.

'You're probably right,' I said.

'I'm *always* right,' said Abs, chucking the pillow back on to her bed. 'It's the hardest thing about being a genius.'

* * *

Even though I'd gone along with Abs and Soph and pretended to agree, I couldn't help feeling there was something seriously fishy about the whole Ruby situation. I was still going over it in my head when Abs's dad dropped me home later that evening.

'Hiya, love,' shouted Mum as I opened the front door. 'We're in here.'

I dropped my stuff in the hall and wandered through to the lounge. Mum and Nan were watching what looked suspiciously like a bad 1970s murder-mystery film. All the men had enormous moustaches and the women were wearing shorts that looked like knickers. Mum's favourite game show, *Soak The Celeb*, was on at the same time, so I guessed Nan had won the what-to-watch argument.

'How did it go?' said Mum, eagerly.

I flopped down on the sofa and filled her in on everything that had happened at the studio.

'So when will you get the CDs?' asked Mum.

'Tuesday. Abs's mum's going to drive us over after school,' I said.

'My little Rosie, on a CD,' said Mum, sniffling. 'Following in my footsteps.'

'Lovely,' said Nan. The credits were rolling at the end of her film. 'You'd never have thought it was that nice boy with the curly hair who murdered the poor girl, would you?' she said, nodding at the TV. 'Of course, he's bald now. I saw him in an episode of *Miss Marple* last week.'

'Nan,' I said, suddenly realising all the television she watched might actually come in handy, 'do you know anything about Ruby Munday?'

'It's the day before Shrove Tuesday,' she said.

'Pancake Eve, you might call it.'

Sometimes, I could swear I was adopted.

'Ruby Munday's a person, Nan, not a date on your *Biscuits of Britain* calendar.'

'She was a film star, wasn't she?' said Mum. 'Sweet little thing with pigtails and a big gap between her front teeth.'

'That's right!' said Nan, nearly knocking over her teacup. 'That group wrote a song about her. What were they called? The Strolling Gnomes? Stoning Trolls?'

'The Rolling Stones,' said Mum.

'Yes,' said Nan. 'They were always a bit loud for my liking. I much preferred the other ones. The Beagles.'

'The *Beatles*,' said Mum. 'Anyway, that song wasn't about Ruby Munday. It was called "Ruby Tuesday". She was named after the song.'

'Then why isn't she called Ruby Tuesday?' said Nan.

'Because her surname's Munday,' said Mum patiently. 'If her parents had called her Ruby

Tuesday, she'd be Ruby Tuesday Munday.'

'Oh,' said Nan. 'So who are the Strolling Gnomes?'

I wonder if I am too old to be adopted now.

'I'm going to bed,' I said loudly, faking a yawn. Sometimes it just isn't worth trying to get any sense out of adults. Talk about doing your head in.

'You've had a long day,' Nan sympathised.

'Recording *is* exhausting,' Mum agreed. 'I can't tell you how often I've come home from a day in the studio and slept for hours and hours. . .'

I left them to it before my brain exploded.

I *could* actually tell you how often Mum's come home 'exhausted' from a day in the studio – twice, because that's the precise number of times she's been in one. I don't remember her being tired when she got back, unless she was sleep-talking through all the endless yawnsome stories.

As I got ready for bed, I couldn't stop thinking about Ruby Munday and her mysterious disappearing act. Why didn't anyone else seem remotely interested?

Chapter Four

Our drama teacher, Mr Lord, is a nightmare on skinny white legs. I won't go into how I know his legs are both skinny and pale (let's just say I haven't been at Borehurst Baths on a Saturday afternoon for a while), but the nightmare bit is mostly down to *Doctor Who*. Time Lord, as he is unfondly known around here, played a Cyberman in the original TV series. He never stops going on about it and, in his tiny brain, he thinks it means he knows everything about acting and films and celebrities and 'the business' as he so annoyingly calls it. The extra joy on top of all this is that we now have him for double drama every Monday morning, ever since our timetables were changed at the start of term.

'Morning all,' he said, strolling into our classroom the Monday after we recorded our CD.

There was a bit of bored 'good morning, Mr Lord' mumbling as he walked over to the teacher's desk and we all resigned ourselves to another hour of Cyberman stories. He hooked his horrible cord jacket over the back of the chair, slung his briefcase on the floor and dropped a newspaper on the desk. Unfortunately, due to me having a majorly huge hair crisis and Soph needing to help me sort it out, we'd arrived about ten seconds before Time Lord, and the only seats left were right at the front. That meant we were unlikely to get away with any snoozing, doodling or sneaky gossiping. On the unexpected plus side, it meant I had an excellent view of the newspaper on his desk. It was open at the entertainment section – *Steve Starman's Celebrity Scoops* – and I couldn't help sneaking a quick peek. To my complete surprise, there was a photo of Ruby Munday right in the middle of the page. Not Ruby the child film star we'd seen in all the pictures on the Internet, but Ruby looking exactly like she had when we'd met her on Saturday. I craned my neck and squinted my eyes, desperately trying to read the upside-down headline over the picture, but before I could, Time Lord snatched the newspaper away. He'd obviously seen me looking at it. I leaned back, expecting the worst – probably a lecture about how focused great actors are and why it's a matter of life and death that they pay attention every last second of the day – but instead Time Lord held the paper up so the whole class could see it.

'What Rosie has spotted is something you'd all do well to note. The entertainment business is not just about talent – it's about attitude, dedication and hard work.'

Blah, blah, blah. Get to the good bit, brain-ache.

'Everything matters,' Time Lord droned on, 'including the way you treat the little people.'

'What, pixies and leprechauns?' Soph whispered.

I hid behind my rough book so Time Lord couldn't see me laughing.

'Behaving like a prima donna gets you nowhere,' he said. 'Status has to be earned in the world of show business. This girl, Ruby Munday, might have been in a few films, but it's no excuse for throwing tantrums and making demands.'

Me and Soph looked at each other. That didn't sound right.

'The first rule of The Business,' said Time Lord, who makes up a new 'first rule' at least once a week, 'is: be good to everyone, even the little people. If you treat *them* badly on the way up the ladder of success, they'll treat *you* badly when you come crashing back down it again.'

Good grief.

He folded up the paper and took out the Shakespeare play we were working on. I still didn't have a Scooby Doo of a clue what he'd been on about, or what it had to do with Ruby. I was itching for the lunch bell to ring so we could check out the newspaper for ourselves.

'"Missing Munday's Diva Demands",' Abs read over my shoulder as we stood outside the newsagent's an hour later.

'What are they on about?' said Soph.

'Duh,' said Abs. 'If we knew that, Rosie wouldn't just have spent half her lunch money on a newspaper.'

'"In an exclusive report, your *Daily News* reporter, Steve Starman, can reveal that former child star Ruby Munday is working on a spectacular showbiz comeback",' I read out loud. '"The actress, who mysteriously disappeared from the public eye almost ten years ago, has reinvented herself as a singer and is determined to be a star once again. But if reports from the studio where she is currently recording are to be believed, all is not going as well as Miss Munday had hoped. In fact, just this weekend, she threw what sources describe as a hissy fit and stormed out of the studio, demanding to be left alone. Rumours are rife that this tantrum is just the latest in a long line of similar outbursts. There is even speculation Ruby's diva demands were behind her sudden departure from the movie industry."'

Abs pulled the tab off the can of cola she'd just bought. 'It's rubbish, isn't it? Ruby was nothing like that when we met her. That reporter's just making it up.'

'But why would he do that?' said Soph. 'Why be mean just for the sake of it?'

'It sells newspapers,' said Abs wisely.

My brain was whizzing. 'How did Steve Starman find out where Ruby was, and who told him she's recording an album?'

Abs and Soph went quiet.

'If she's been missing for all that time, how did the newspapers suddenly manage to track her down?' I said.

'Someone must've told them,' said Abs, realising what I was getting at. 'Someone must have phoned up and said they knew where she was.'

'But why?' said Soph.

'That's the easy bit,' I said.

'Money,' Abs nodded.

'The hard part is working out who.'

'Hang on a minute,' said Soph. 'Aren't we forgetting something?'

'What?'

'When Steve Starman, or whoever, found out where she was, why did they decide to write all this bad stuff about her?'

'It does seem weird,' I said. 'I mean, she was so cool when we talked to her.'

Abs took the paper off me and started reading again.

'It's not fair,' said Soph. 'Papers just write what they like and get away with it.'

'You know what else is a bit weirdy-beardy?' said Abs. 'If you read the article, it's not totally untrue. Ruby *did* come out of the studio because she wanted to chill on her own for a while. She said it herself.'

'No way was it a hissy fit, though,' I said.

'I know,' said Abs. 'It's just odd that they're making things up, but sort of basing it on the truth.'

'I still don't get it,' said Soph. 'If that reporter found out where she was, why didn't he phone up and ask her to do an interview? They'd have got a story without having to make anything up.'

'Sacré bleu!' I said, making them both jump. 'Soph, you're brilliant. *The Daily News* didn't do an interview with Ruby, but maybe I could.'

'For *Star Secrets*?' said Abs.

I nodded. Ever since I landed this amazing scoop when I was on work experience at *Star Secrets*, Belle, the editor, has let me write loads of cool stuff for them. Getting Ruby Munday to tell her side of the story in the magazine would be huge. I was half surprised I hadn't thought of it sooner.

'I'll call Belle when I get home after school,' I said, 'and if she says I can do it, I'll ask Ruby when we go to pick up the CDs tomorrow.'

✵ ✵ ✵

NosyParker: Just phoned Belle. Ruby interview is on!

FashionPolice: Yay!

CutiePie: What did she say?

NosyParker: That I am a genius.

CutiePie: What did she REALLY say?

NosyParker: 'Rosie, you are amazing. An interview with Ruby Munday would totally rock and we will pay you handsomely for it.'

CutiePie: How much is that exactly?

NosyParker: You will never know, mon amie.

FashionPolice: Come on. Spill.

NosyParker: I will never know either. Mum puts it all in a dullissimo savings account for me.

CutiePie: Unfair!

NosyParker: Si, si, signorina. But that's parents for you.

FashionPolice: So are you going to ask Ruby tomorrow?

NosyParker: Do the French eat snail sandwiches?

Chapter Five

The following afternoon, Abs's mum drove us back to Fleetwich to pick up our CDs.

'See what I mean about normal?' I said to Abs as we drove along. Her mum had just put the new Fusion song on and was humming along. 'If this was Mum's car, we'd be listening to Radio Time Warp and trying not to breathe in the smell of those half-mint, half-toffee things she eats when she's driving.'

'My mum might have OK taste in music,' Abs whispered, 'but look at the kind of rubbish she likes reading.'

She pulled a folded-up magazine out of her school bag and passed it to me.

'*True Life Stories?*' I said.

Abs nodded. 'She loves it. They make her all snivelly and emotional.'

'What are you doing with it?'

'I bought it in the newsagent's this morning,' said Abs, still keeping her voice low as Soph and Mrs Flynn sang along to Fusion in the front. 'I'm going to give it to her when we get to the studios. If she's reading this, we can take as long as we like to pick up the CDs and you'll have plenty of time to talk Ruby into doing the interview.'

Abs is what les Français call une grande genius.

* * *

'We might have to wait a while for them to . . . er . . .' said Abs, as we clambered out of the car twenty minutes later.

'. . . put the covers on the CDs,' I said, helpfully. 'You know, make sure we're happy with the photos.'

'Take as long as you like,' trilled Abs's mum. 'I've got plenty to keep me busy.' She patted the cover of *True Life Stories*, then pulled a seriously huge chocolate bar out of her handbag and opened the magazine.

'We're pretty much invisible to her now,' said Abs cheerfully.

I still hadn't quite worked out how to ask Ruby about the interview, or even how we were going to find out if she was at the studios, but I was sort of hoping Nadia might help us out. She'd been really friendly, and considering she was such a huge Ruby fan, I guessed she'd be totally into my plan to set the record straight. But when we walked into reception, it wasn't Nadia sitting behind the desk, it was Will. He looked up and gave us a brain-meltingly gorgeous grin.

'Hey!' he said. 'It's Borehurst's hottest new girl group.'

'That's us,' said Soph.

'What can I do for you?' Will asked.

'We're here to pick up our CDs,' Abs told him.

'Nadia said they'd be ready today.'

He looked around the desk. It was a bit like those cupboards you see in designery magazines – so mega-hip and sleek, the doors and drawers don't have any handles and anyone who doesn't have a degree in cupboardology can't actually work out how to open them.

'I'm sure they're here somewhere.' He lifted up a few piles of paper in a useless sort of way. Like forty CDs would be hiding under a couple of sheets of A4.

'I don't s'pose you'd mind waiting around for a few minutes?' he said, looking a bit embarrassed, but still utterly gorgey. 'I'm looking after the desk for Nadia. She had to go out, but she'll be back any time now.'

'No problemo,' said Abs, giving me an 'aha!' kind of look. There was a definite whiff of cunning plan in the air. 'Is there a loo we could use while we're waiting?' she asked Will in her most charming voice.

'You only went half an hour ago,' said Soph. She

is not that great in the cunning-plan department. Abs gave her the death-stare.

'It's not for me,' she said, gritting her teeth. 'Remember how Rosie's had a bad stomach all day? She said in the car she needed to go – you never know what might happen if she has to wait until we get back to Borehurst.'

WHAT?

Will looked alarmed. Abs would have done, too, if she'd known what I was thinking.

'It's down the corridor,' he said. 'Next door to the chill-out lounge.'

'Thanks,' said Abs, striding off in the direction Will was pointing. Me and Soph followed.

'There's extra paper on the shelf if you need it,' Will called after us.

'Abs,' I said as soon as we were out of earshot, 'I may very well have to kill you.'

'Me?' she said. 'If Soph had kept her lip zipped, I wouldn't have had to say anything.'

'I don't get it,' said Soph. 'Who needs the toilet?'

'No one,' said Abs. 'But I spotted it in this bit of

the corridor at the weekend, and it gives us a good excuse to sniff around and see if Ruby's here.'

'In the loo?' said Soph, still clueless.

'I give up,' said Abs.

'Hello,' said a voice behind us.

'Ruby!' we said with one voice, all turning round at the same time.

She laughed. 'I'm glad someone's pleased to see me.'

'Course we are,' I said. 'Why wouldn't we be?'

'I thought you might've read all that stuff in the newspapers,' she said, her face falling. 'Loads of people are avoiding me at the moment – like they think I might be about to throw a tantrum or something.'

'We did read it,' I said, 'but it was totally obvious they'd made it up.'

'We were telling this girl at school – a complete troll named Amanda Hawkins – about meeting you,' said Soph, 'and how you weren't anything like what the papers have been saying.'

'Thanks,' said Ruby, brightening up a bit. 'So,

what are you three doing back here?'

'We came to pick up our CDs,' Abs explained.

'Nadia's not at her desk, though,' said Soph. 'And Rosie's got a bad stomach, so we're taking her to the loo.'

'THERE IS NOTHING WRONG WITH MY STOMACH!' I said, maybe a bit too loudly.

The door to Ruby's studio opened, and the man with the black hat stuck his head out again.

'Everything all right, Rubes?'

'It's fine,' said Ruby. 'I was just about to ask the girls if they wanted to come in and have a quick listen to the stuff we've been working on.'

'Seriously?' I said.

'Course,' said Ruby. 'I told you the other day, it's really important I get the songs right – I want to know what you think of them.'

'It must be really hard,' I said, as we followed her into the studio. 'I mean, all the pressure, with everyone expecting you to make a huge comeback and be totally successful again.'

'It was bad enough before,' she said, 'but all

that stuff in the papers is making it even worse.'

I was just about to dive in and ask her about my interview when the man in the black hat handed her a CD.

'This is Aidan, my producer,' she said, and slipped the CD into a player under the mixing desk. 'And this is a kind of sampler we put together last week of all the songs that are definitely going to be on the album.'

She pressed play and the studio was filled with the sound of Ruby's voice. She had been a brilliant actress, but by the sound of it she was an even better singer. She bit her lip and watched us closely as the CD played about half a minute of each song, then faded into the next one.

'I love it!' said Soph, as the CD finished.

'It's awesome!' I agreed. 'Especially the second-last song.'

Ruby and Aidan smiled at each other. "Someone Else's Life",' said Ruby. 'We think that's going to be the first single.'

'When's it coming out?' Abs asked her.

'It'll be a while yet,' said Aidan. 'A couple of months, probably.'

He glanced up at the clock on the wall.

'Yeah,' said Ruby, catching his eye. 'We should get back to work. Sorry,' she said. 'It was great to see you again, though, and I'm glad you liked the songs.'

'We're definitely going to buy the album,' Soph assured her.

'Thanks,' said Ruby. 'At least I'll have three fans, even if the newspapers put everyone else off.'

'Ruby, about the newspapers and the bad publicity,' I said, feeling nervous all of a sudden. It was now or never. 'I was kind of hoping we'd bump into you today.'

'OK,' she said slowly.

'It's just, I'm sort of a reporter, too. Well, not for the newspapers or anything, and I don't make stuff up like that Steve Starman bloke, but I have done a few interviews for *Star Secrets* and they've said I can do one with you. I mean, only if you agree, obviously, but I thought you might want to tell your side of the story.'

Zut alors! How much was I going on?

SHUT UP, BRAIN!

'Sure,' Ruby said, shrugging. 'I wasn't planning to do any interviews until the album's finished, but considering the papers are already writing about me, I may as well. At least this way, it'll be with someone I trust.'

Oooh, I'm good.

'Cool,' I said, like celebs tell me that kind of stuff all the time.

She went to get her diary so we could work out a good time, and I tried not to do my famous celebration dance while Aidan was watching.

✳ ✳ ✳

'Hiya,' said Nadia, as we walked back into reception. 'Will said you were here. Did you find the spare toilet rolls?' she asked me sympathetically.

'Yes, thanks,' said Abs quickly.

'I've got your CDs here,' Nadia said.

'We've been talking to Ruby,' I chipped in,

determined not to let everyone think I'd just spent fifteen minutes in the loo with an exploding-bottom problem.

'Ruby?' said Nadia, handing Abs a cardboard box full of CDs.

'We saw her in the corridor,' I explained.

'What were you talking about?' said Nadia.

'All sorts,' Soph chipped in. 'The newspaper stories, her album . . .'

'Me interviewing her for *Star Secrets* magazine,' I said, bursting to share the news.

'*Star Secrets*?' said Nadia.

I explained about work experience and all the writing I've done for Belle since.

'Belle thought it was a great idea,' I said, 'and Ruby did too. It'll be a chance for her to let people know the truth – what she's really like.'

'Right,' said Nadia.

I carried on. 'She was totally into the idea of getting some good publicity.'

'Well, what Ruby wants, Ruby always gets,' said Nadia.

I was a bit shocked. Had Nadia meant to sound so catty? On Saturday, she'd hardly stopped going on about how great Ruby was.

'We should probably go,' said Abs, breaking the awkward silence. 'The effects of my mum's chocolate bar will be wearing off any minute now. Thanks for the CDs,' she said to Nadia.

'I'll see you on Friday afternoon,' I added.

Nadia looked a bit confused.

'I'll be back to do the interview,' I said.

'Oh.' She smiled. 'Cool. I'll see you then.'

Chapter Six

You can always tell something's up when Amanda Hawkins sits down next to you and smiles. It's a bit like this documentary I accidentally saw about vultures. If you see a vulture, it's a sure sign there's a dead body nearby, belonging to some poor ex-animal. Amanda Hawkins's smile is a sure sign there's doom in store for someone within tormenting distance.

'All right, Nosy?' she said, plonking down next to me with a grin, at lunchtime on Thursday.

Oh joy.

'I suppose you've heard this,' she said, waggling her mp3-player about in front of me. 'Seeing as you're *such* good mates with Ruby Munday.'

'Heard what?' I said.

'Her attempt at a song,' said Amanda, gleefully. 'It's all over the Internet.'

'Any time you want to start making sense, Amanda,' said Abs, 'you go right ahead.'

'How thick are you?' Amanda sneered, which was totally the pot calling the kettle a loser, or whatever that saying is. 'This,' she said in the kind of slow, shouty voice tourists use when they're trying to make French people understand English, 'is a MA-CHINE that plays SONGS. One of the SONGS on it is off the IN-TER-NET. It is by RU-BY MUN-DAY and it is RU-BBISH.'

'Yeah, right,' I said. Even if Ruby was the most amazing singer Amanda had ever heard, she'd still say she was awful just to annoy me, Soph and Abs.

'We listened to a whole bunch of her songs the other day and they were brilliant,' said Soph.

'Says the tone-deaf fashion freak,' said Amanda

to her cronies, Lara Neils and Keira Roberts, who were lurking behind her. They laughed, which, quite frankly, they would do even if their bottoms were on fire. They are that stupid.

'If you don't believe me, listen to it yourself,' said Amanda, standing up. 'I'd let you hear it on this,' she added, holding up the mp3-player again, 'only I wouldn't want to catch anything off the headphones.'

'Like what?' I called after her. 'Brain cells? A decent sense of humour?'

'Sacré bleu, she's annoying,' said Soph.

'Soph, that's like saying my nan is barking,' I said. 'Totally obvious and a massivo understatement.'

We all sat there, half-heartedly picking at our lunch. I knew Abs and Soph were just as desperate as me to find Ruby's song on the Internet.

'Library?' said Abs eventually.

'Si, si,' I said, grabbing my bag, 'and don't spare the horses.'

* * *

'It's probably a marketing thing for her album,' said Abs as we sat down at one of the computers in the school library. 'Loads of pop stars leak songs on to the Internet on purpose.'

'Why?' said Soph.

'Publicity?' I suggested.

'Exactly,' said Abs. 'It gets them masses of attention. People get really excited about hearing one or two songs for free, and by the time the album comes out, they're totally desperate to buy it.'

'Sneaky,' said Soph.

'Is there anything you don't know, Abs?' I said.

She grinned as I typed Ruby's name, then 'mp3' into the search engine.

'Have you got your mp3-player with you, Soph?' I whispered. Miss Donovan, the librarian, had just walked past.

'Oui,' said Soph, pulling it out of her bag. 'Why?'

'I need the headphones. We can't very well crank up the volume in here, can we?'

I clicked on one of the links I'd found, and Soph plugged her headphones into the computer. 'You go first,' she said, passing me the headphones.

I pulled my hair forwards so they were hidden and played the song clip. It was 'Someone Else's Life', the song Ruby had said was going to be her first single, only it didn't sound like the version we'd heard in the studio. When it finished, I passed the headphones to Abs, then she passed them on to Soph.

'That is seriously weird,' I said when we'd all heard it.

'What?' said Soph.

'You didn't think it sounded . . . well . . . different?'

'Try dreadful,' said Abs.

'No,' said Soph.

'Put it this way,' I said, 'that song sounds like someone's been taking singing lessons from you.'

'It is still Ruby, though, isn't it?' said Abs.

'Sounds like it,' I said. 'Just a really out-of-tune version of her.'

'I don't get why she'd leak something if it was that bad,' said Soph.

'Unless someone else leaked it,' said Abs.

'Someone who's trying to wreck her comeback!'

'But who?' said Soph.

'The same person who sold the story to the newspapers,' I suggested.

'Brilliant,' said Abs. 'Or it would be if we had any idea who that actually was.'

'You know what you said about it sounding like me?' said Soph. 'I was just thinking – Will made me sound like I've got a really good voice when we were recording our CD.'

'You don't mean . . .' I said.

'No way,' said Abs.

'She's got a point, though,' I said. 'How do we know Aidan hasn't been using pitch correction on all Ruby's songs?'

'We don't,' said Soph. 'We haven't heard her singing live, just on that CD.'

'And now this,' said Abs, pointing at the computer.

It was a horrible thought.

Which was Ruby's real voice?

The next afternoon, me and Mum drove back to Fleetwich so I could interview Ruby. Considering she'd practically had to beg her boss, Vile Vincent, to take two hours off work, Mum was in a surprisingly good mood. I had a horrible feeling she was planning something. We were, after all, going to a studio full of musicians and producers, and she is nothing if not obsessed with singing. Her bag looked suspiciously bulgy, like it was crammed full of demo CDs.

'Blimey,' she said as we pulled into the courtyard. 'It's a bit bigger than the studios I'm used to.'

'Both of them?' I said under my breath.

'What's that?'

'I've got you a present,' I said.

She turned the engine off as I pulled a magazine out of my bag and handed it to her.

'*True Life Stories?*' she said.

'And this.' I handed her a bar of chocolate. 'To

say thanks for driving me. I thought you could wait out here and read the magazine while I do the interview.'

OK, so it was a long shot.

'That's lovely,' said Mum, 'but it's not really my cup of tea. Who wants to read about life when you could be out there living it?'

Everyone else's mum, that's who.

She opened the door.

'Come on, you don't want to be late.'

'Mum,' I said, as we walked into reception. 'You won't embarrass me, will you?'

'Of course not,' she said. 'What d'you think I'm going to do?'

Ooh, I don't know. Off the top of my head, maybe wear electric-blue leggings, admit you're in a tragic eighties tribute band, tell people you're my mum – the usual stuff.

I didn't say any of this out loud in case she got all narky-parenty on me, which would only make things worse.

'Rosie,' said Nadia, spotting me. 'Hi.'

'Hi,' I said.

Mum cleared her throat in a over-the-top way.

'Nadia, this is my mum,' I said, dully.

'Nadia,' said Mum. 'What a pretty name. I'm Liz.'

She stuck her hand out and Nadia shook it a bit warily.

'Well, this is all a bit grander than I'm used to,' said Mum. 'I'm a musician myself,' she added, obviously thinking Nadia's silent codfishy expression meant she needed an explanation rather than an escape route. 'A singer,' said Mum. 'I'm in a band – the Banana Splits?'

Nadia didn't say anything.

'We've done loads of gigs in Fleetwich. You've probably seen the posters,' said Mum. 'A big yellow banana, split in half down the middle, with me and the girls peeping out –'

'So, is Ruby around?' I said, loudly. Sometimes it's just easier to talk over Mum and hope she gets the hint. 'I'm here for the interview.'

'Yeah, I know,' said Nadia, looking a bit awkward. 'The thing is, she's had to cancel.'

'Oh,' I said.

Mum had wandered off and was peering down the corridor towards the studios.

'How come?'

'She's taken the day off,' said Nadia. 'You've seen how hard she's been working. She's exhausted. She said she needed a break. You know, before she burns out.'

Just when I thought things couldn't get any weirder. Ruby had seemed so up for doing the interview, and I'd thought what with the leaked mp3, she'd be even keener to get some good publicity.

'I'm really sorry,' said Nadia. 'We didn't have your phone number, and neither did Ruby, otherwise we'd have called to let you know.'

'What's wrong?' said Mum, coming up behind me.

'Ruby couldn't make it,' I said. 'The interview's cancelled.'

Mum frowned. 'Doesn't she want to do it any more?'

'It's not that,' I said. 'She just isn't here today.'

'Why don't you leave her a note?' Mum suggested. 'Ask her to give you a ring and arrange it for another day.'

'You'll have to drive me here again if I do that.'

'It's fine,' said Mum. 'Not a problem.'

Any excuse to come back and find someone worth pestering, I thought.

As she pulled a notebook and pen out of her handbag, I caught sight of what was unmistakably a Banana Splits CD.

'Here you go,' she said. 'Write her a note on this, and leave it with Nadia.'

Half-wondering if it was the first good idea my mum had ever had, I scribbled a message for Ruby, wrote my phone number at the bottom, tore the page out and folded it in half.

'Will you give this to Ruby?' I asked Nadia. She looked at me blankly. Then I heard footsteps coming along the corridor and someone walked into the reception area. It was Aidan, Ruby's producer.

'Hi,' he said, smiling.

'Hi,' I replied. 'Erm, could you possibly give this note to Ruby for me?'

'Sure. Absolutely. I'll pass it on as soon as I see her,' Aidan agreed.

'Thanks,' I said, relieved that at least someone at the studio was on the ball.

'You're totally welcome,' he said, tucking the note into his pocket as he turned to greet what appeared to be a very cool-looking rapper and his entourage who'd just arrived.

'See you soon, yeah?' Nadia beamed as me and Mum left.

* * *

'She,' said Mum, as we walked back out to the car, 'is quite a peculiar girl.'

Chapter Seven

By the time Monday morning arrived, the Ruby situation had got more out of hand than my nan's obsession with *Murder, She Wrote*. On Saturday evening, Soph phoned to ask if I'd seen the papers.

'Oh, yes,' I said. 'The first thing I do when I hit the mall on a Saturday afternoon is head straight for the newsagent's to stock up on newspapers. No boring clothes shops or record stores for me.'

She gave me her mum's favourite lecture about sarcasm, then told me to go and look up the online versions of the papers. The stories were all about

Ruby, they were all totally bad and things didn't get any better when the Sunday papers came out.

Ten things the weekend newspapers said about Ruby (but which are so not true):

1. 'In a desperate bid to save her career, Ruby Munday has signed up to appear on *Celebrity, Clean That House!* next month.'
2. 'Ruby's album is on track to become the slowest-selling CD in history.'
3. 'Everyone who worked with Munday on a movie set was forced to call her "Miss Ruby", and her contracts always demanded dressing rooms be painted ruby-red and filled with bowls of ruby-red fruit every day.'
4. 'Queen of the Hissy Fit, Ruby threw a pizza at an innocent delivery boy last week because there were too many anchovies on it.'
5. 'Snubbed by the acting community and ridiculed by the music world, Ruby Munday is a laughing stock.'

6. 'Anna Bilson, a former classmate, claims Miss Munday's singing voice was so bad when they were at school together, Ruby was forced to mime to hymns in assembly.'

7. 'Ruby's most successful career move was her sudden and dramatic disappearance from the limelight, and it looks like the public are demanding a repeat performance.'

8. 'Currently considering plastic surgery to regain her cute childhood looks, Ruby Munday's life is in meltdown.'

9. 'Fame-hungry Ruby Munday plans to launch her own perfume, clothing line, look-alike dolls and even a range of Ruby pasta sauces.'

10. 'Ruby Munday abducted by aliens!'

'Who writes that junk anyway?' I moaned to Soph in registration on Monday morning. 'And why haven't any of them bothered to get a proper interview with Ruby?'

'I know,' said Soph. 'They were talking about her on breakfast TV this morning, too.'

The whole thing had just been more lies and rumours.

'She still hasn't rung you, then?' said Soph.

I shook my head. The more I'd seen false stories about Ruby, the more obsessed I was with checking my phone to see if she'd got in touch. I'd even spent ten minutes staring really hard at the phone, sending vibes out across the universe to Ruby, *willing* her to ring me. She didn't, and I got a bit of a headache from all the concentration.

'D'you reckon she's going to call?' said Soph. 'Like, at all?'

'If she doesn't, I'm going back to the studios next weekend and staying there until she talks to me,' I said.

'Wow,' said Soph. 'What are you going to wear?'

That is Soph all over. Not 'how will you get there, oh wise and courageous Rosie?', or even 'how can you force her to talk to you?' (neither of which I was especially clear on, actually).

'That's not the point,' I said, very patiently. 'A good reporter does not give up so easily, especially when it could be the scoop of the century.'

'Isn't that a TV show?' she said.

'What?'

'Scoop of the century.'

'Focus, Soph,' I said. 'I've made a plan for today, and the rest of the week if need be, but I can't do it on my own.'

'Oooh, I love your plans,' said Soph.

'Thank you.'

I pulled my phone out of my school bag and held it under the desk so Mr Adams, our très handsome form teacher and soon-to-be boyfriend of my mum (that was another plan altogether) couldn't see what I was doing.

'You aren't meant to have that switched on in here,' said Soph.

'Exactamundo,' I said. 'But what if Ruby calls and it's switched off and she forgets to leave her number on my voicemail because she's too upset, or she leaves it and it doesn't record properly, or I accidentally delete the message before I've heard it? Then she'll just think I don't want to interview her any more because I've started believing the newspapers. If it rings, I've got to answer it.'

'If it rings, you'll be in detention faster than Abs can say her fourteen times table,' said Soph.

'When I say "ring", I mean vibrate,' I said. 'It's on silent. I'll feel it shaking as soon as a call comes through, and that's where you come in.'

'Ah, oui,' said Soph. There was a pause. 'How?'

'When I give you the signal, you stick up your hand and tell the teacher I'm about to be sick and you've got to get me to the loos,' I explained. 'I'll make the sick face,' – I blew my cheeks right up and wrinkled my forehead to show her – 'and hold my stomach. You lead me out of the room, and then I can answer the phone.'

'Signal – hand – sick – loos – leave the room,' said Soph. 'Got it.'

'Sure?'

'What's the signal?'

By some miracle, it actually worked – probably because my phone rang in the next lesson, which meant Soph hadn't had time to forget the plan.

Ruby didn't sound at all like her usual happy self when I picked the phone up, but I was getting a bit nervy standing out in the corridor during lessons, so I couldn't exactly say much or ask her anything.

'Half past four tomorrow?' she suggested when I asked about rearranging the interview.

'Cool,' I said, relieved she still wanted to do it.

'I'll see you then,' she said.

* * *

Which was how I found myself standing in the Icon Studios reception yet again the following afternoon with Mum. I hadn't even bothered trying the magazine-and-chocolate trick this time. When we got there, Nadia was really busy, but she rang through to Studio B to let Ruby know I'd arrived and told us to take a seat.

'You can't come in while I'm doing the interview,' I told Mum as we waited.

'That's fine,' she said. 'Plenty to keep me amused out here.'

'Like what?' I said, suspicious.

'You never know who you'll bump into in an interesting spot like this,' she said, looking around.

The reception area was really busy, and I had a sudden, horrible vision of Mum handing out Banana Splits CDs to anyone and everyone the minute I left her alone.

But before I could start begging her to sit still and be normal, Ruby showed up.

'Hi,' she said.

Mum leapt up so fast, Ruby actually jumped.

'Ruby Munday,' said Mum, grabbing one of Ruby's hands between both of hers and shaking it like a madwoman. 'I'm Liz. Liz Parker. Rosie's mum. It's an honour to meet you.'

'You, too, Liz Liz Parker,' said Ruby.

'Oh! HA, HA, HA!' Mum laughed. She was so loud that everyone in reception was staring at us.

As much fun as I was having, standing there dying slowly of embarrassment, I decided the interview was more important.

'Ruby's really busy, Mum,' I said, imitating Abs's best death-stare, 'so we're going off to do the interview now.'

'Surely she's not too busy to –' Mum started.

There was an enormous possibility that sentence would have ended with the words 'listen to one of my Banana Splits CDs', so I took drastic action to save Ruby from a fate worse than bad publicity.

'Isn't that man over there a really famous record producer?' I said. While Mum was busy sticky-beaking at him, I grabbed Ruby's arm and pulled her along the studio corridor.

* * *

I hadn't been in the chill-out lounge before, but it was really cool. The walls were painted a cosy kind of dark purple and were almost completely covered in old concert posters. There were four squashy mismatched sofas scattered around the room, plus several holey-looking chairs and a massive stack of CDs and music mags. I spotted a fridge in one corner, and next to it there was a small sink, a kettle and a tottery pile of cups.

'Sorry about my mum,' I said, as Ruby got us some drinks.

'She seems really friendly,' said Ruby.

'You don't have to live with her,' I said.

Ruby passed me a bottle of juice and settled down on the sofa opposite.

'So, how are things?' I said.

Ruby's face fell for a second. 'Oh, you know,' she said.

'Not everyone believes what they read in the papers,' I said.

'That's what Aidan keeps telling me. He says I should ignore it and get on with recording the album.'

'Isn't that really hard when you've got all this on your mind?' I asked.

'Totally,' she nodded. 'But he says once everyone

hears the songs, they'll forget the lies and rumours, and the music will speak for itself. Cheesy, eh?' she added with a grin.

'As a stilton-and-mozzarella sandwich,' I agreed.

'Fire away, then,' she said. 'Although I might be rubbish at answering. It's been ages since I've done an interview.'

'When was the last one?' I said.

She thought for a minute.

'Just before the premiere of *Don't Tell Dad*,' she said. 'Wow, that is a long time.'

No point beating round the bush, Rosie, I thought. She brought up the subject of her last film – dive straight in with the big question.

'So, what happened after that?' I said. 'Why did you stop making films?'

Ruby went really quiet.

'It's a long story,' she said. 'There were all kinds of reasons. It just . . . happened that way.'

'Oh.'

I was a bit surprised that she'd gone all quiet. Still, like I'd told Soph, a good reporter doesn't give up that easily.

'What about all that time since? Where were you – what were you doing? It's been, like, nine or ten years, hasn't it?' I said.

She nodded. 'Just, y'know, growing up, I suppose. Normal stuff.'

Good grief. It was harder than getting conversation out of Nan when the TV was on. I flipped through the pages of my notebook to look for a safer question. At this rate, Belle would be lucky to get enough for two lines on the gossip page.

'Music!' I said. 'I mean, your comeback – how come you've decided to do music instead of going back to films or acting?'

She sat forward and smiled. 'It's what I was meant to do,' she said. 'I've loved singing since I was really young. Mum says I sang before I learned to talk. The first time I ever earned any money from acting – it was for a TV commercial – Mum and Dad let me buy a piano, and that was it. I started writing songs a few years later, and obviously I did all that stuff like singing into my hairbrush . . .'

And on, and on, and on. She was totally back to chatty, friendly Ruby. As long as I stuck to questions about what she was doing now, and general things like her fave food or TV shows, she talked and talked, but the minute I mentioned her past, she went weirdy-beardily silent. I was starting to get brain-ache again. It was obvious Ruby was hiding something, and just as obvious she wasn't about to tell me what. I'd been so sure she was the cool, funny, friendly person we'd met the first time we'd been at the studios, and that all the rumours were just made up, but there were too many things that didn't make sense. I was really starting to wonder if Ruby was what she seemed.

※ ※ ※

When the interview eventually ended, she hugged me and I promised to send her a copy of the magazine as soon as it came out.

'Thanks again,' I said, as she headed back to Studio B. She was working on another new song with Aidan, and I thought about asking if I could listen. I was pretty sure the pitch-correction thingy only worked *after* you'd sung something, and I really wanted to hear Ruby singing live. But I didn't want her to think I was getting suspicious. If I was going to find out the truth, I needed a plan, and that meant finding an excuse to come back and dig around some more.

I sat there sorting out my notes and thinking. Maybe I could convince Mum to pay for another recording session.

'DON'T DO IT!' shouted my brain. Like she'd be able to resist tagging along and forcing me to join in with some hideous duet.

I opened my bag to shove in the notes and my mini-recorder, and my homework diary fell out. *Bingo, and oh yes! Make way for another brilliant Rosie Parker plan.* I shoved the diary under a cushion, making sure the corner was poking out just enough for someone to spot it.

Smirking, I picked up my stuff and headed off to reception. It was up to me not only to solve the mystery of Ruby Munday, but also to save the producer-population of Icon Studios from my mum and her bag of CDs.

Chapter Eight

'Again?' said Mum, when I got off the phone with Nadia the next afternoon.

I'd called the studios to ask if anyone had found my homework diary cos that was the last place I remembered seeing it. My surprise and relief when Nadia told me she'd got it was so convincing, I half wished Time Lord had been there to see it.

'What's that?' said Nan, padding into the kitchen.

'Rosie needs driving over to Fleetwich again,' said Mum.

'What for?' said Nan.

'I left my homework diary behind after the interview yesterday.'

'Can't they post it to you?' said Nan.

Brilliant. The one sane thought Nan's had all year, and it has to go and mess up my entire plan.

'No,' I said quickly. 'No . . . er, it wouldn't be safe. It could get lost in the post. School would go mad if I lost it. They'd probably make me do, like, the whole term's homework all over again, and then I wouldn't have time to revise, and I'd fail my exams and I'd probably end up working in Bigger Burgers for the rest of my life.'

Nan is nothing if not easily alarmed.

'Are you sure you shouldn't drive her over there now, Liz?' she said to Mum.

'Tomorrow will be fine,' Mum said, scraping a frozen piece off the chicken she'd been cooking for the last half an hour. 'And it had better be the last time.'

* * *

For someone who'd been totally desperate-issimo to come to the studios a few days ago, Mum was suspiciously irritable as we pulled into the courtyard again.

'Look at that,' she said, nodding towards a group of men standing just outside reception wearing band t-shirts and baggy jeans.

'What?'

'Haven't they got anything better to do than just hang around?'

'I thought you said the people here were interesting.'

She switched the engine off. 'They might be,' she said. 'But they're not very friendly.'

'What, because none of them have offered you a record deal yet?' I said. Actually, I didn't say it out loud. It was a very long walk back to Borehurst.

Mum followed me into reception, mumbling something under her breath about people not knowing talent when they heard it.

'Hiya,' said Nadia, spotting us. She'd been

chatting to someone who was leaning on the reception desk, and I realised it was Will.

'Hey, Rosie,' he said.

Swoon-a-rama.

'Are you feeling better?'

'I, um . . .'

'Better?' said Mum. 'What was wrong with her?'

'Toilet trouble,' said Nadia.

'She had a lot of that when she was younger,' Mum told them. 'We used to call her Rosie-Poo. She was nearly four by the time we got her potty-trained. I'm Liz, by the way,' she added, beaming at Will.

'Rosie's mum,' he said. 'I've heard a lot about you.'

Oh, good grief.

'I'm Will,' he said. 'I produced the CD Rosie and her friends recorded.'

'Really?' said Mum, who totally looked like she'd left her sense of shame in the car. 'You did a marvellous job, especially on poor Sophie.'

'Maybe Liz would like to have a look round the studio,' said Nadia. 'See how you work your magic.'

Quite surprisingly, Will didn't run away screaming. I gaped as the two of them headed off down the corridor.

'He loves showing the studio off,' Nadia explained, 'and I got the feeling your mum was interested when she was here the other day.'

'Try mega-desperate,' I said.

'Here you go,' said Nadia, handing me my homework diary. 'You left it in the chill-out lounge.'

'Thanks,' I said. 'It must've dropped out of my bag when I was interviewing Ruby.'

'Oh, right,' said Nadia, like she'd forgotten all about the interview. 'How did that go?'

'Fine,' I said. 'I emailed the finished article to Belle last night and she loved it.'

'So it's going in the magazine?' said Nadia.

I nodded. 'Next week.'

'It's about time Ruby had some good press,'

said Nadia. 'She deserves a break.'

'That's why I wanted to do the interview,' I said. 'When you meet her, it's so obvious all those other stories are made up. She's not a diva.'

'I know,' Nadia agreed. 'And it's not like everything's been easy for her, either. Growing up in the limelight was a nightmare. Everyone thinks it must be so cool hanging out on movie sets and being famous, but most of it's just boring. She was really lonely.'

'Didn't she have friends on set?' I said.

'Sometimes, I suppose,' Nadia shrugged. 'You're mostly hanging round with grown-ups, though. And then,' she said, lowering her voice, 'after slogging away to make all those films, the studio fired her because she wasn't cute enough any more. No wonder she disappeared. It must have been seriously humiliating.'

'I guess,' I said. I'd never really thought of it that way before.

'That's why I got out of it,' said Nadia. 'Acting is just too harsh.'

'You were an actress too?' I said, surprised.

'Yep,' said Nadia.

'Why did you give up?' I said. 'Surely it's better than being a receptionist.'

'Not really,' she said. 'You spend half your time going to auditions and getting told you aren't good enough for jobs you didn't even want in the first place. Then, when you do get a part, it's in some stupid advert, or just being an understudy. Anyway, this isn't my real job. Well, it is, but only for now. I'm a singer.'

'Wow. What kind of stuff do you sing?'

'Eighties, mostly,' said Nadia. 'Like your mum.'

Sacré bleu and, as les Français also say, zut alors.

'Cool,' I said, weakly.

Nadia grinned. 'I'm joking, silly! I like the same kind of bands as you, remember? – Mirage, Sugababes, that kind of thing.'

'So, do you do gigs or anything?'

'Sometimes,' said Nadia. 'It's really hard to fit it in around my job here, though. I've just started recording an album, so sometimes I hang around after I've finished and they let me use one of the studios.'

'You must be really talented,' I said, wondering how to get the conversation back on to Ruby. It wasn't that I wasn't interested in what Nadia was talking about. I just hadn't come all the way here to find out her life story.

'I came top of my year at stage school, if that counts as talented,' said Nadia.

'Stage school?'

'Yep. Emilia Halliwell's Academy of Dance and Drama,' said Nadia. 'We did singing as well, but it was too much of a mouthful to add it to the name.'

Something was nagging at the back of my brain as she talked. I had a weird feeling I'd heard that name somewhere before.

'. . . must be nearly ten years now,' Nadia was saying. 'I've still got my tap shoes, though, and obviously the voice training is really useful at the moment. Did you hear that?'

'What?'

She didn't answer. In the silence, I could hear a strange sound.

'It's coming from the corridor,' said Nadia, moving out from behind her desk.

Please, I thought, following her, *do not let it be my mum*. It was bad enough that Will had now had plenty of time to work out where my bonkers streak came from without adding any extra embarrassment.

But it was soon obvious where the noise was coming from and it wasn't my mum. I only had about a millisecond to feel relieved, though.

'Ruby?' I said.

She was standing outside the door to the chill-out lounge, sobbing, with a screwed-up newspaper in her hand. She looked up as I hurried over to her.

'Rosie.' She seemed confused. 'Hi.'

'Are you OK?' I said, which is officially the stupidest question in the world to ask a crying person.

She tried to say yes, but her face crumpled and

she started sobbing again. I turned round to Nadia, who was just standing there, watching.

'Let's go in here,' I said to Ruby, putting one arm round her shoulders and pushing the door open with the other.

She let me lead her into the chill-out lounge and sit her down on one of the squashy sofas. I got her a bottle of water and as I walked back across the room, I saw that Nadia had followed us in. She sat gingerly on one of the sofas opposite while I plonked down next to Ruby and put my arm around her again.

'Was it something in the paper?' I asked.

She nodded and handed it to me.

'RUBY MUNDAY COMEBACK ALBUM VOTED WORLD'S WORST' screamed the headline. '(AND IT HASN'T EVEN BEEN RELEASED YET)' said a second, smaller row of print underneath. It was so obviously rubbish, I didn't even bother reading the rest.

Next to me, Ruby blew her nose and rubbed her eyes with the back of her hand.

'Sorry,' she sniffed. 'I'm being stupid. I should be used to it by now.'

'What? People telling lies about you all the time?' I said.

She gave me a watery smile.

I looked over at Nadia, thinking it might be good if she joined in with the whole you'll-be-OK-don't-pay-attention-to-the-stupid-papers thing, but she had the weirdest expression on her face, like she was watching a film instead of a real, crying person right in front of her. As soon as she realised I was watching her, she came over to sit on Ruby's other side.

'You'll be fine,' she said, patting Ruby's arm. 'The papers will move on to someone else in a few weeks, and no one will remember any of this.'

Ruby sniffed again.

'Thanks,' she said. 'It's nice to know there are some people who still believe in me.'

The thing was, I wasn't entirely sure Nadia was one of them.

Chapter Nine

As soon as we got home, I headed upstairs to my room. I was desperate to see what I could find out about Emilia Halliwell and her stage school. I threw my homework diary into my schoolbag, took my shoes off and turned my computer on. As I waited for it to boot up, my brain drifted back to Ruby. She'd seemed OK by the time I left. Mum and Will had found us in the chill-out lounge and joined in with trying to cheer her up, and Nadia had gone back to reception. I sort of got the feeling she was relieved to be going. I wondered if it had anything to do with her being such a big Ruby fan. Loads of people got a bit tongue-tied and awkward around their idols. If you'd followed someone's career since they were five, it must be a bit weird to have them sitting right in front of you with a puffy red nose and their eyes swollen up like pink marshmallows.

The search engine beeped into life and I typed in the name of Nadia's stage school. Their web site was mucho hilarioso – lots of pics of girls wearing pastel-coloured leotards and smiling so hard it looked like the corners of their mouths were tied to their ears. There were lots of references to 'our lovely little ladies' – ew. Apart from the comedy value, though, there was nothing that helped me remember where I'd heard the name before. Did I even know anyone else who'd been to stage school?

And then it hit me – Ruby!

The first time we'd looked her up, there'd definitely been something on one of the sites about a stage school. I quickly typed in 'Emilia

Halliwell's Academy of Dance and Drama' again, and this time added 'Ruby Munday'. But there were no results. Frowning, I tried just 'stage school' and Ruby's name.

Bingo!

I clicked on the link and scrolled down the page. I was pretty certain this was the same site I'd looked at with Abs and Soph. It took a second, but then I found it:

> Before being spotted by Hollywood film agent, Dirk DeMauro, Ruby was a popular student at the Isobel Chester School of Performing Arts.

Bum. I'd been so sure that was it. I hit the 'back' button, wondering if there was any point looking up Ruby and her amazing disappearing act again. The search-engine page filled the screen, replacing the Ruby fan site, and as it did so, I noticed another one of the results, a bit further down the page. My heart leapt as I saw the name 'Emily Helliwell'. One mouse-click later and I was on a page that finally looked like it could get me somewhere. It was an old newspaper article, and as I read, my heart started beating faster. Ruby had gone to the Isobel Chester School of Performing Arts, just like the first site said, but Isobel Chester and Emilia Halliwell – or Emily Helliwell as this newspaper article had called her – were huge rivals. They'd both opened stage schools at around the same time, and the schools had been in fierce competition ever since. The article must have been written before Ruby got really famous, because she was only mentioned once, as a young pupil who'd just starred in a TV advert. The article was about the schools' rivalry and some of the dirty tricks Isobel and Emilia got up to. The fact they kept calling her Emily instead of Emilia must have been why I didn't find the article the first time I searched.

I flopped back on my bed. If the two schools were rivals and the pupils were rivals too, did that include Ruby and Nadia? I suddenly remembered something Nadia had said earlier on – 'it must be nearly ten years now' – which meant she'd been at stage school at exactly the same time as Ruby. Suddenly, the mystery-solving bit of my brain whizzed into action. If Ruby and Nadia were somehow rivals, or even enemies, it was easy to see all the stuff that had been going on in a completely different way. The papers finding out where Ruby was and what she was doing, the rumours about her diva-ish behaviour, the leaked sound-clip, even my interview getting cancelled – the one person connected to all of those things was Nadia. The more I thought about it, the more it totally made sense. Convinced, I sat up. It was time to call for reinforcements.

NosyParker: You know when you know that you know enough to work something out?

CutiePie: I don't even think I know enough to work out what you're on about.

FashionPolice: You should sooo see this new top I'm making.

NosyParker: I think I know who's been trying to sabotage Ruby.

FashionPolice: You lie!

NosyParker: Au contraire, mon frère.

CutiePie: Spill!

NosyParker: It's Nadia. She and Ruby were rivals at stage school. I think she phoned the papers when R started working at the studios.

CutiePie: Sacré bleu!

FashionPolice: Exactement. I bet it was her who leaked the song, too, and cancelled my interview.

FashionPolice: We so have to tell Ruby.

CutiePie: If we come over now, we can phone her from yours.

FashionPolice: Yay! I can wear my new top.

NosyParker: Soph, you are so shallow.

I think Ruby was quite surprised when we called her. From the amount of times I'd turned up at the studio since the first time we met her, I might have been starting to seem like a mad stalker.

When Abs and Soph turned up, I showed them what I'd found on the Internet and told them my Nadia theory again. As Abs pointed out, it still didn't solve the whole Ruby mystery, but at least it might help put a stop to all the evil newspaper stories about her.

Together, the three of us explained to Ruby what we'd found out, and what we thought had been going on.

'I don't understand,' said Ruby. 'You're saying Nadia's been doing all this just because she was at Halliwell's and I went to Chester's?'

'I'm not sure,' I said. It did sound a bit feeble when you put it like that.

'Even if that's not the reason why,' said Abs, 'the rest of it still makes total sense.'

'Nadia could easily have phoned the papers,' I said.

'And she told you it was hard working as a receptionist when she wants to be a singer,' Abs chipped in, 'so she might be taking money from the papers, hoping to give up her job.'

'I suppose,' said Ruby, still sounding doubtful.

'She's been working at the studios in the evenings as well,' I carried on, 'which would've given her chance to steal your CD *and* make it sound really bad before she leaked it.'

'Kind of like backwards pitch correction,' Soph added.

'And you said something about the interview on Friday?' said Ruby.

'She said you'd taken the day off because you were exhausted and you'd cancelled the interview,' I told her.

'That's not true,' said Ruby, indignantly. 'Nadia told me you'd phoned on Friday morning to cancel, so I went home early to work on some lyrics.'

'That proves it, then,' said Soph. 'She was lying to both of you.'

'It's horrible,' said Ruby.

We all made agreeing noises.

'I guess I'll have to talk to her,' said Ruby.

'Give her what for, more like,' said Soph.

Ruby giggled.

'I don't suppose . . . ' she said, slowly, 'I know it's a lot to ask, but I think she might be more likely to confess if you're there, too. We can all tell her what we know, and she can't lie to me about what you've said, or the other way round.'

'No problemo,' said Soph.

'We'll be there with bells on,' Abs added.

'Sure,' I said, wondering how on earth I was going to convince Mum to drive us to Fleetwich again.

* * *

'You've got to do it,' said Nan, a few minutes later when we went downstairs to ask Mum. 'You can't leave poor Robbie to confront the villain on his own, not when these three have done all the hard work solving the mystery.'

'It's Ruby,' I said. 'And she's a she, not a he.'

'That's what I said,' said Nan. 'Come on, Liz,'

she added turning back to Mum. 'Do it. In the name of Mystery.'

'Fine,' Mum sighed. 'I'll take you.'

Nan smiled. She loves getting her own way.

'I knew you'd see sense,' she said, patting Mum's hand.

She winked at me, Abs and Soph.

Yes, winked.

'A successful detective is only as good as his foot soldiers,' she said.

I'm telling you, she is losing her marbles so fast you can practically hear them falling out of her ears.

Chapter Ten

The next morning, me, Soph and Abs met Ruby at the studios about half an hour before Nadia was due to start work. Mum spent the entire journey moaning about the traffic or the weather or the price of fish or something. I wasn't really listening. When we arrived, a man I'd never seen before let us in through a little door at the side of reception.

'This is Miles Harper,' said Ruby. 'He's the studio manager. And,' she added, 'an old friend.'

'My dad directed most of Ruby's movies,' said Miles. 'I've known her since she was an annoying little brat who used to play practical jokes on me.'

Ruby stuck her tongue out at him.

'That's the reason I decided to record my album here,' she explained. 'Miles would never tell anyone I was here, or what I was doing, so I knew I'd be safe.'

'You *thought* you'd be safe,' said Miles. He looked at me, Soph and Abs. 'Ruby told me what you found out about Nadia.'

'And you believe us?' I said.

'Absolutely,' said Miles. 'I just want to go through it again before Nadia gets here to make sure I've got the facts straight.'

For what felt like the hundredth time, I went through the whole story, with Soph, Abs and Ruby chipping in every now and again. Miles nodded a lot and asked a few questions, all the time his expression getting more and more grim.

'So, what's the plan?' I said, once we'd told him everything.

'We wait for Nadia and confront her,' he said simply.

'You're a bunch of early birds,' said Nadia, dropping her handbag behind the desk and shrugging her coat off.

'I wouldn't bother doing that if I were you,' said Miles.

'Oh, bum. Is the heating broken again?' She pulled the coat back on and then stopped. 'Am I missing something? What are you all staring at?'

'The game's up, Nadia,' said Miles. 'We know what's been going on.'

Nan would have been mucho impressed by his cheesey cop-show lingo.

'I'm glad someone does,' said Nadia. 'What are you on about?'

'You've been trying to sabotage Ruby's comeback,' said Miles.

'Me?' said Nadia. 'How?'

'Telling the papers where she was, passing on fake stories about her,' said Miles.

Nadia laughed. 'You're winding me up, right?'

Miles shook his head. 'You knew where Ruby was and you had access to the studios. You could easily have leaked that mp3 on to the Internet.'

'Yeah,' said Nadia. 'But so could you. So could anyone working here. Why am I being blamed?'

I had that feeling again, like it was all sounding a bit far-fetched, but there was still a bit of my brain that *knew* Nadia was behind all of this.

'Your behaviour, things you've said about Ruby, just don't add up,' Miles told her.

'And that's it, that's your evidence?' said Nadia. She laughed again. 'I don't believe this. I could sue you for making false accusations.'

'What about my interview?' I said, suddenly remembering. Me and Ruby were both here now. She couldn't deny she'd lied to us.

Nadia stared at me. 'I don't know what you're talking about.'

'You told Rosie and Ruby two different lies about that interview,' said Miles.

'I got confused,' Nadia shrugged. 'I had a headache.'

I looked at Miles, willing him to keep believing our story and find a way of proving it.

'So, you're saying you had nothing to do with it,' he said, slowly. 'You didn't phone the newspapers to tell them Ruby was working here?'

'No, I didn't,' Nadia snapped. 'And unless there's anything else you want to accuse me of, I've got work to do.'

'Sure,' said Miles. He leaned over the reception desk and picked up the phone. 'You don't mind do you?' he asked Nadia. 'I just need to make a quick call to my mate Dave at *The Daily News* and see what he can tell me about the person who's been feeding them all the Ruby stories.'

I was pretty sure Miles's friend Dave was made up, but it was still an impressive move.

Nadia froze.

Miles started dialling the number.

'Fine,' said Nadia.

Miles stopped dialling and waited.

'OK, I told them she was here,' said Nadia. 'But so what? You can't prove anything else.'

'Apart from the fact you also told the papers a bunch of lies about Ruby having hissy fits,' I said.

'I might've known you'd have something to do with this, Little Miss Ace Reporter,' Nadia spat. 'You think you're so clever.'

'You told the papers, after I made it clear to everyone how important it was that we respected Ruby's privacy?' said Miles.

'I needed the money,' said Nadia.

'That doesn't explain why you told them lies,' said Miles.

'You could easily have said good stuff about Ruby,' I added.

'OK!' Nadia threw up her hands. 'You want the truth? I did it. The papers, the mp3 clip, messing up your interview – all of it. And I'm not sorry.'

'But why?' said Ruby.

'You really don't have any idea, do you?' said Nadia. 'All those years when we were at stage school, going up for the same parts. You never knew who else had auditioned, because you were always the one who got the parts. I went from one miserable audition to the next, not getting anywhere, and then there you'd be a few months later on TV or in some film, playing another one of the parts I didn't get.'

Ruby didn't say anything.

'I hated you,' Nadia continued. 'I still hate you.'

'But you said you'd given up acting,' I pointed out.

'Why would you want to get back at me for something that happened such a long time ago?' asked Ruby.

'Because you're still doing it,' said Nadia. 'Still stealing my thunder. I gave up acting to be a singer. I'm recording an album. But what happens? Who comes along to do exactly the same thing and take it away from me?'

'So you decided to get your revenge,' said Miles.

'Why shouldn't I? Ruby had no idea who I was. Ringing the papers and spreading a few rumours was easy. I only did it a couple of times, then they started making stuff up for themselves.'

'And the mp3?' said Miles.

'Master keys,' said Nadia, jingling the bunch she'd just used to get in through the main entrance. 'There's one to every studio here. I hung around until Ruby and Aidan left one night, then sneaked in and burned a copy of their sample CD. I used some pitch correction, uploaded it to the Internet and voilà – everyone finds out just how overrated Ruby Munday is.'

'Except that's not her real voice,' I said.

'Whatever,' sighed Nadia.

'I think we've heard enough, don't you?' said King of Cop-show Clichés, Miles, looking round at me, Abs, Soph and Ruby.

He held his hand out to Nadia with the palm facing upwards.

'Nadia, the keys,' he said.

She dropped them angrily into his hand.

'Nadia,' he said, pointing towards the entrance, 'the door.'

'What?' said Nadia.

'There is the door; I would like you to go through it,' Miles repeated.

'I don't –'

'YOU'RE FIRED!' Miles bellowed.

* * *

'That totally rocked,' I said, flopping down on to one of the sofas in the chill-out lounge.

'You were awesome,' Ruby told Miles.

'Very cool shouting,' agreed Soph.

'Nadia only got what she deserved,' said Miles, handing round some chocolate biscuits he'd found in the fridge. 'In fact, she probably deserved a lot worse than getting sacked after what she did to Ruby.'

'She's gone,' said Ruby. 'That's what really matters.'

'Apart from the fact all the papers still think you're one hissy fit away from totally losing the plot,' said Abs.

'Thanks,' laughed Ruby.

Abs clapped a hand over her mouth. 'I didn't mean . . . sorry. It's just, *we* know Nadia made all that stuff up, but the papers have no idea. She might be going off to sell them another pile of lies.'

There was a squirming sort of silence.

'There is one way we could make sure everyone else knows the truth,' I said.

Ruby looked at me.

'*Star Secrets*!' we both said at the same time.

'I'll have to ask Belle,' I said, thinking. 'She might think it's too soon for another interview, but I bet she'd put something in the magazine.'

'Ring her,' said Ruby. 'Go on. It's not like it would be just another interview, anyway. It's your story – you solved the mystery.'

'Another exclusive by ace reporter, Rosie Parker,' grinned Soph.

'And –' Ruby started to say something, but then seemed to change her mind.

'What?' I said.

For some reason she looked at Miles.

'It's about time, Rubes,' he said.

'The reason I disappeared,' she said, looking back at me.

Oh yes, I am a legend.

'I know I was a bit cagey the last time, but if Belle says you can do another interview I promise I'll tell you everything. I want people to believe the truth about me, so I've got to tell them everything, be totally honest.'

'No more mysteries,' said Miles.

'And you're really going to let me be the person who gets the story?' I said. 'Out of all the journos and reporters and TV chat show hosts in the world?'

'I told you, it's yours,' said Ruby. 'Totally exclusive. You've earned it.'

I took out my mobile and scrolled through the address book at top speed. I had to do this before she changed her mind.

'Belle,' I said, 'it's Rosie. You are not going to believe this.'

✳ ✳ ✳

If my life was a film, this would be the bit where the screen goes all funny and then shows a caption saying 'two weeks later'. If my life was a film, I would also have a much smaller bottom, a much bigger bedroom and less-mad relatives. But sadly, this is real life, so as well as putting up with my bum, my boxroom and my bonkers Nan, I am stuck with just saying 'two weeks later'.

'"Ruby Munday: The Whole Truth",' Mum read as Nan scraped a layer of marmalade on to her toast. '"Music, revenge and the real story behind her mystery disappearance. World exclusive by Rosie Parker".'

Belle had sent me the latest issue of *Star Secrets* a day before it hit the newsagents' shelves so I could see how my article had turned out.

'Saints preserve us,' said Nan, dropping her knife. 'Show me. Where does it say that?'

Mum passed the magazine across the table, pointing at my name.

'That's you!' said Nan, which was stating the très obvious, even for her.

She got a bit soggy round the eyes. 'I'm so proud,' she sniffed. 'It's like I've got my own little

Jessica Fletcher. *Murder, She Wrote*, right here in Borehurst.'

'No one got murdered, Nan,' I said, just about managing not to add, 'and I am not some batty old woman with bad taste in jumpers'. Jessica Fletcher is Nan's style icon.

'Let's have a proper read, then,' said Mum. She swiped the mag back off Nan and started poring over the article. 'Ooh, listen to this,' she said to Nan after a few minutes. '"Ruby says she finds it hard to understand why people are so interested in her disappearance. 'It really isn't the huge mystery everyone thinks it is,' she explains. 'My mum and dad were worried about all the attention I was getting at such a young age. I'd made ten films by the time I was ten years old. Being around film sets, they started to see how fame could mess up the lives of young actors, and they didn't want that for me.'"

'Smashing,' said Nan, nodding. 'Very wise.'

'Ssh,' said Mum. 'Listen. "They decided to take me away from it all so I could have a more normal life and concentrate on school until I was older.

We went to live in New Zealand, where my films had never been released and no one knew who I was. Even though I was happy with my family, and the friends I made at my new schools, I really missed acting and singing. It was a difficult time, but I've put it all behind me now. I don't talk about it much, because I'm happier thinking about the future, and the fact I'm doing what I love again."'

'So that was it,' said Nan. 'Poor little Robbie, too famous too young. Good job his parents were on the ball, eh?'

'It's Ruby,' I said, even though it was pointless.

'It *is* much easier to cope with success as a performer when you're a bit older,' said Mum, thoughtfully. 'I've found that myself.'

Hmmm. Listen to Mum going on about her so-called career as a singer, or leave for school? It was a tough choice.

'I'll see you tonight,' I said, grabbing my books and snatching the magazine off Mum so I could show it to Soph and Abs.

'What about your other letter?' said Mum.

'Other letter?'

'There were two letters in the post for you this morning. The magazine, and another one. I told you when you came downstairs,' said Mum.

'No, you didn't.'

'I did,' she said, rifling through a stack of mail on the kitchen counter. She handed me a small padded envelope. 'You never listen, that's your trouble.'

Honestly, is it my fault if she mumbles?

'I'll open it on the way to school,' I said, waving the package at her and Nan.

I'd just caught sight of an Icon Studios sticker on the back, and I had a funny feeling I knew what was inside.

* * *

'Did you find one?' said Abs.

Soph dropped her lunch tray down on the table next to us.

'Yep,' she said. 'It's Lucy Cameron's. She wants it back straight after the bell, though.'

She took a portable CD player out of her bag and put it on the table in front of me. It was practically as big as my plate.

'Who on earth still has one of these when they could get an mp3 player?' I said.

'Luckily for us, Lucy Cameron does,' said Abs. 'Where's the CD?'

'I still can't believe Ruby finished it so quickly,' said Soph, as I took the shiny new disc out and passed it to Abs.

I'd waited until I got to school to open the envelope because I sort of wanted Abs and Soph to be there, too. Ruby had promised to post us a copy of her album the minute it was finished, and who else would be sending me stuff from Icon Studios? None of us expected it to be so soon, but Ruby had put a note inside explaining that all the time Aidan had spent telling her to get on with recording and ignore the papers had really paid off.

'Once Nadia had gone, I suddenly realised we'd got enough songs and the album was ready,' Ruby had written. 'We added some finishing touches, recorded a few new backing vocals (but you already know about that bit) and that was it.'

'OK,' said Abs. 'Ready?'

She pressed 'play' and we all leaned in to listen through the headphones at the same time.

'Move it forward to track four,' I said, reading the back of the disc.

'Is that the one we're on?' said Soph.

'Ooh! Our debut as backing singers!' said Abs.

We listened in an awed kind of way.

'Wow,' I said, eventually. 'We totally rock.'

'You rock, and I rock, and pitch correction rocks,' said Abs, smirking at Soph.

'I sound seriously amazing,' Soph said. And it was true.

'You sound amazing doing *what*, fashion freak?'

Amanda Hawkins. Perfect timing.

'Oh, you know,' I said, mega-casually. 'Singing backing vocals on the new Ruby Munday CD.'

'As if,' scoffed Amanda.

Lara Neils and Keira Roberts did a bit of their usual halfwit sniggering behind her.

'Surely you're not saying you don't believe us?' said Abs, with a fake shocked expression on her face.

'Nosy might have got lucky when she interviewed her,' said Amanda, grudgingly, 'but there is no way Ruby Munday would let you lot sing on her album.'

'See for yourself.' I threw the booklet part of the CD at her.

'You're looking at page four,' Abs pointed out. 'You see there where it says "Backing vocals: Rosie Parker, Abigail Flynn, Sophie McCoy" and then again in the credits on the back page?'

'"Special thanks to Rosie, Abs and Soph – you're the best",' read Amanda. Her face went from angry red to jealous green in about two seconds.

I smirked. 'I never in a million years thought I'd ever agree with you, Amanda, but for once, you're right. We *are* the best.'

For a minute, it looked like her head might explode, but she just turned round and stalked off.

'You're good,' said Abs.

'Totally twisted,' agreed Soph.

'I know,' I said. 'Just call me a genius.'

Fact File

NAME: Ruby Munday

AGE: 19

STAR SIGN: Capricorn

HAIR: Curly and brown

EYES: Brown

LOVES: Singing live on stage and being true to herself

HATES: Jealous rivals and spoilt divas!

LAST SEEN: Singing in front of a cheering audience

MOST LIKELY TO SAY: 'I'll answer any questions – just don't ask me about being a child star!'

WORST CRINGE EVER: Leaving her microphone on while she went to the loo. The whole studio heard her wee!

Soph's Style Tips

**No cash shouldn't equal no style!
Here's Soph's fashion guide for babes**

STYLE SURVIVAL CHECKLIST

- ☑ High street shops have great designs

- ☑ Charity shops are top for vintage gear

- ☑ Supermarket fashion is cheap as chips

- ☑ Customising old stuff is really funky

- ☑ Swapping with mates is totally FREE!

- ☑ Accessorising can change your style!

GOING CHEAP!

OK, so you've seen this totally cool dress in a magazine but it's all like, 'model wears dress by blah-de-blah, one zillion pounds', and you're thinking 'how am I ever going to get a zillion pounds before Saturday?' It's every girls' dilemma, but don't be put off! You can totally get the same look for loads less money. Hit the high street with determination. There are loads of designer-inspired styles in budget shops. And check out supermarket clothes shops, too. If you look for long enough, you'll find a similar dress for heaps less. Good luck!

FASHION MAGIC!

Listen up, style disciples! This is the tip I like to call, 'how-to-make-one-outfit-into-loads-of-different-looks' and it's very useful for babes on a budget, so you don't want to miss it. OK, so say you've got a plain T-shirt and a denim skirt, right? That's outfit number one. But now try wearing a belt over your T-shirt and you've got sophisticated look number two. Or if you want some Saturday style, throw on a few bright plastic necklaces. Numero tres! Never underestimate the power of accessories for they are the budget babe's best friend.

SWAP YOUR STYLE

If your purse is full of air, you're not alone! Talk to your friends and explain the situation. Half the time, me, Rosie and Abs never have any money, so don't stress! Instead of going shopping, just get swapping! Set a date and each bring along some tops, skirts, jeans and accessories. Then have a big trying-on session and borrow something cool from your mates. Wearing something different is just as good as having something new! Well, almost. And you get to hang out with your friends, just like you do on a shopping trip. Problemo solved!

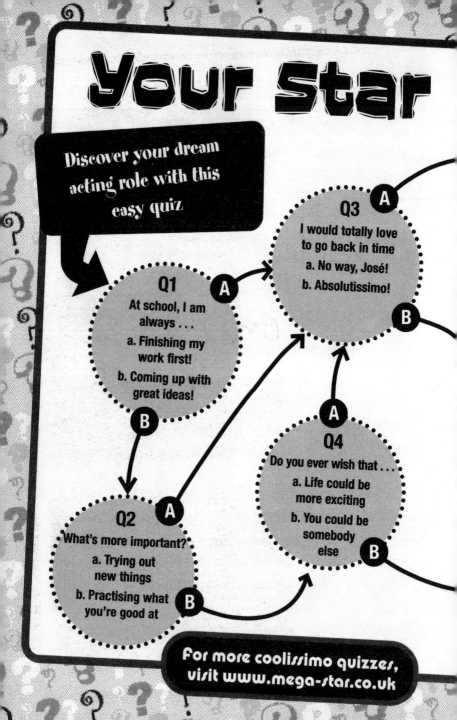

Act

Soap Celeb

Forget life in the fast lane. That's way too slow! You live your life at the speed of light! You're just the girl to play a main character in a top TV soap. You love change and excitement and you're adaptable too. You'd be perfect! And with your fantastic memory, learning all those lines would be a breeze!

Most likely to say: 'My character is totally not guilty . . . this week, at least'

Q5
Can you remember your friends' birthdays?

a. Every single one!

b. Only if I write them down!

A

B

Film Star

Ring-ring! Hollywood calling! There's never a dull moment in the movies! You'd totally love it! You'd get the chance to play lots of different roles and work in loads of new places. Acting in films would be a great way to show the world how versatile you are. Not to mention all the glamour and fame!

Most likely to say: 'Give me variety. I don't want to get typecast!'

Q6
What would be your perfect outfit?

a. It depends what kind of mood I'm in

b. A long floaty dress!

A

B

Drama Queen

Well, grab yourself a bonnet and bat your eyelashes! You were born to play the heroine in a costume drama. All those hours in hair and make-up wouldn't bother you at all! You'd do anything to bring your story to life! Swooning into the path of handsome heroes would be all in a days work!

Most likely to say: 'Er, is there a horse standing on my skirt?'

Megastar

Everyone has blushing blunders - here are some from your Megastar Mysteries friends!

Ruby

I went on a chat show to talk about my album, but the host was far more interested in my childhood acting days. I finally brought the conversation back to music and offered to sing my new song, 'Rock Bottom'. I was so happy to be performing at last that I didn't notice they were playing a clip behind me on a big screen. As I hammered out the chorus, I turned round and saw a massive image of myself, starring in a nappy advert, aged two. My baby bum was magnified to the size of a double-decker. Talk about shameful!

Rosie

Me and Abs were going to the corner shop and Nan asked if I would get her some garibaldi biscuits. You know, the kind with the squashed flies? Well, they're not really flies, they're raisins. But anyway, off we went to the shop. I couldn't spot them, so I cheerfully asked the shopkeeper if he had any garibaldis. Just that second, I noticed he was wearing a name badge that said 'Gary'. Then I clocked his very bald head. Oui, mes amis, I actually asked bald Gary for some garibaldis. Next time, Nan is sooo getting digestives!

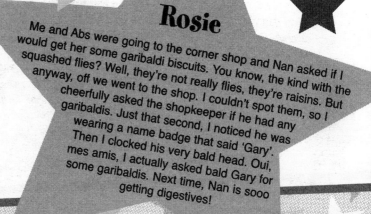

Cringes

Abs

I'd been in town for ages, trying to find a present for Megan's fifth birthday. I was just starting to feel desperate, when I spotted a Pink Princesses annual in the window of the bookshop. The perfect Megan present, right before my eyes! I rushed inside, grinning with relief. But just as I grabbed the book, Amanda Hawkins appeared out of nowhere. She rolled her eyes over the babyish annual in my hands and sniggered her way out the door before I could explain. Crrrrrrrringe!

Sophie

We were having a fashion show at school and I was so excited! I'd been practising my runway walk for a week, so when it was my turn to strut out on stage, I really went for it. I marched to the end of the stage and did a high kick to demonstrate all the fabulous layers in my skirt. As I jumped up, my shoe flew off. It hurtled though the air like a rocket and crash-landed in Mr Adams lap. Très, très un-*Vogue*.

Pam's Problem Page

Never fear, Pam's here to sort you out!

Dear Pam,

I want to be a singer but things keep going wrong. I can't help thinking that someone is trying to sabotage my career. Could and old rival be to blame or am I just paranoid?

Ruby

Pam says: Oh, dearie me, love. It does sound like you're in a pickle! I suggest you close your eyes and put yourself in Jessica Fletcher's shoes. The heroine of Murder, She Wrote would take a spot of sabotage in her capable stride, and so can you with a bit of help! Try to imagine that you are a top lady detective, just like Jessica. You'll work out who your rival is in no time. Then just tell your town sheriff what's what. He'll take it from there. Good luck, duckie!

Can't wait for the next
book in the series?
Here's a sneak preview of

Pulse

Chapter One

If there's one good thing about the drama lessons at our dull school, it's that they're not the science lessons at our dull school. Really – that's as good as it gets. This is partly down to the teachers. Mr Lord – Time Lord, as we call him – is our so-called drama teacher, although he mostly just goes on about how he once played a Cyberman in *Doctor Who*. Our science teacher, Mr Footer, is in training for the title of World's Most Boring Man, and he's doing very well. He also has a moustache that looks like a slug. When all's said and done, it's the slug that clinches things in the rubbish-teacher stakes, but it's a close-run thing.

So, when Time Lord stood smugly in front of our drama class one Monday morning and said he'd got an important announcement to make, nobody exactly sat up and looked interested. Not that a bunch of bored faces has ever stopped Time Lord from droning on before.

'As most of you will remember, I trained at an excellent drama school before joining the cast of *Doctor Who*, then taking on a number of other challenging stage and television roles,' he began.

'That'll be "excellent", meaning the only place that'd take him,' whispered my best mate Abs, who was sitting next to me and my other best friend Soph near the back of the drama studio.

'And "a number of" meaning two,' I added.

We sniggered as Time Lord carried on.

'One of my fellow graduates, Jim Falconer, is a film-maker, and he's been looking for a location for his latest project, *Pulse*. Naturally, I was one of the first people he called for advice and, thanks to my years of experience in the world of film and television, I was immediately able to help him out. The film is a musical, written by Jim himself,' he added, going into what Abs calls his 'actor-mode'. He basically gets all over-dramatic with this wild, looking-into-the-distance expression and lots of long pauses. It's mucho hilarioso. 'It's a classic story of misguided youths, a passionate, brilliant teacher and how even the greatest of problems can be solved through music and dance.'

Good *grief*.

'A group of unruly pupils,' said Time Lord, and I swear he squinted over in my direction, 'are thrown together by their headmistress to organise a school dance, in a last-ditch attempt to stop their bad behaviour. Rivalry, love interest,' he went on, 'it's all there. All of human life.'

He looked around the room, obviously expecting us to be enthralled, or impressed, or something. No one was, so he carried on, a bit less actor-ish, but still with this mega-smug expression on his face.

'Anyway, once Jim had filled me in on the details,

I had a brainwave. A musical set in a school? Why, here at Whitney High would be the perfect location! I could be his inside man, and even take on one of the film's smaller – but most vital – roles. Strictly as a favour to an old friend,' he added, hastily.

'How much d'you reckon he begged?' Soph said, under her breath.

'Bribed, more like,' I grinned.

'So, of course, Jim jumped at the chance of offering me a part in his film, as well as the opportunity of using Whitney High as the location,' Time Lord finished.

I had to admit, this was starting to sound way cooler than the stuff he normally comes up with. Exactly fourteen people saw our last drama class play (it was about a misunderstood dentist), and I'm pretty sure Time Lord paid most of them to turn up. Even Mum and Nan – who'll usually sit through any old rubbish – made excuses not to come.

'They're going to make a film right here in our school?' said Abs, doubtfully. It did seem too good to be true.

'Not just a film, Miss Flynn, a *musical*,' said Time Lord, dreamily. 'I've always been a big fan, myself. *West Side Story*, *Guys and Dolls*, *My Fair Lady* – all the greats. I was once likened to a young Gene Kelly by a reviewer in the *Biddlesbury Reporter*, you know.'

'Where's Biddlesbury?' asked Abs.

'And who's Gene Kelly?' said Soph.

Time Lord looked totally shocked.

'Who's Gene Kelly?' he echoed. 'Surely you've seen *Singin' in the Rain*?'

He stared around the group and we all shook our heads blankly.

Five things that happened in the next twenty minutes:

1. Time Lord gave us a lecture on the geniusness of this actor called Gene Kelly and a bunch of other film stars who are now either very old or very dead.

2. Time Lord filled us in on the entire plot of *Singin' in the Rain* (so there's no point actually

watching it now cos we know exactly what happens).

3. Time Lord borrowed Frankie Gabriel's umbrella.

4. Time Lord and Frankie Gabriel's umbrella demonstrated the famous scene where Gene Kelly sings and dances in the rain.

5. Time Lord leaned on Frankie Gabriel's umbrella to kick his tap-dancing feet up in the air. Frankie Gabriel's umbrella broke, and possibly one of Time Lord's toes did, too.

'As I was saying,' puffed Time Lord, hobbling back to his desk, 'I was one of the few pupils at the Elizabeth Meakins School of Dance and Drama who could sing, dance and act all at the same time. It's a skill very few performers ever perfect, but those of us who are blessed with the ability feel obliged to share it every once in a while.'

Seriously, it can't be good to hold in a laugh as big as the one I was stifling. I made the massivo mistake of looking at Abs, and nearly exploded.

I turned my spluttering into a coughing fit and Soph thumped me on the back.

'Is there a problem, Rosie?' said Time Lord.

'We were just wondering, sir,' Abs managed to squeak, 'if you know who'll be appearing in *Pulse*?'

'Well, Jim's keeping most of the stars' identities a secret until we start filming,' he said, clearly enjoying the fact we actually seemed interested in what he was saying for once. 'But, of course, I've already let slip that yours truly will be amongst the big names on set, and a little show-business bird told me Estelle Mayor will be joining us, too.'

'Estelle!' said Soph.

'You might remember her from the television talent show, *Stage-Struck*,' said Time Lord.

Well, duh! We might also remember her from the time me, Abs and Soph reunited her with her mum's famous long-lost brother on live TV in yet another triumph of mystery-solving genius.

'And there'll also be the chance for a few of Whitney High's most talented drama students to join the cast as extras,' Time Lord continued.

There was a definite hum of excitement in the air now. I looked excitedly at Abs and Soph. We sooo had to do it!

Time Lord raised his voice. 'For those of you who are interested, I'll be holding auditions next week, although,' he added, looking at Amanda Hawkins with a barf-making smile, 'these will merely be a formality for some people.'

Amanda is totally Time Lord's pet pupil, as well as being my sworn enemy and the class witch. She gets the lead in every play we do, even though she's useless and can't act her way out of a carrier bag, or whatever that saying is.

But no *way* was I going to let Amanda Hawkins ruin news like this.

'This is the single most exciting thing ever to happen at Whitney High,' I said meaningfully to Soph and Abs the minute our lesson ended.

'This is the ONLY exciting thing ever to happen here,' Abs corrected me. 'We are going to audition, right?' she added.

'Do the French eat frogs' legs?' I said.

'We'll have to work out what we're going to sing,' said Abs.

'And a dance routine,' I agreed.

'Clothes!' said Soph.

'Yeah, I was thinking I'd wear some,' I said.

'You can't just wear them,' she said, sounding horrified. 'There's all the thinking about them, and planning, and making new stuff. And we've only got a week!'

I should explain that Soph, in case it's not stunningly obvious, is obsessed with fashion.

* * *

By the end of the week, the entire school was buzzing with news, gossip and wild rumours about the filming. A girl from year eleven swore she'd overheard Time Lord telling Madame Bertillon that Orlando Bloom was actually a brilliant singer and dancer and had agreed to star in *Pulse* so he could finally reveal this to the world. Becky Blakeney, who's in the same form group as me and Soph, told us she'd heard one of the stars had left to join a death-metal band and they were planning to pick a replacement from the people who went to Time Lord's auditions next week. And then, just when you thought it couldn't get any weirder, Luke Bailey from the year above us started saying Jim Falconer didn't exist and it was actually Time Lord (in disguise) who was going to be making the film.

'Yeah, right,' scoffed Abs when we found out, 'as if Time Lord's a good enough actor to pull *that* off.'

'You know what *is* true, though?' said Soph. The three of us had just plonked ourselves down in our usual seats in the canteen, and I knew Soph was as desperate as I was to tell Abs the juicy bit of gossip we'd overheard at the end of morning break. 'Amanda Hawkins is having extra coaching sessions every lunchtime.'

'*Drama* coaching,' I added, just to make sure Abs understood the enormousness of the news. 'With Time Lord.'

'No *way!*' Abs's jaw practically hit her plate of chips.

I nodded, quite smugly. Gossip rocks.

'How is that fair?' said Abs. 'Why should Amanda Hawkins, of all people, get more of a chance than the rest of us?'

'That's what we thought at first,' said Soph, 'but then Rosie pointed out . . .'

'. . . that Time Lord's not exactly wowing big movie producers at auditions every day of the week,' I joined in.

'For all we know, he could be so bad he's wrecking Amanda's chances instead of improving them,' said Soph.

A surprisingly evil grin spread over Abs's face. 'Oui, oui, mes amis,' she said. 'You might just be right.'

'Hey, who's that with Meanie Greenie?' I said, suddenly spotting our headmistress coming into the canteen with a tall, scruffy-looking man.

'Ladies and gentlemen,' shouted Mrs Green, before Abs or Soph had chance to answer. 'If I could just have a moment of your time,' she clapped her hands, and the canteen fell silent. 'As I'm sure you're aware, Whitney High is to be used as the setting for a film during our summer break this year. Earlier today, I had the pleasure of meeting Mr Falconer, the film's director,' – she gestured at the scruffy man – 'who's here to look around and get a feel for our school building. And, in order to clear up some of the silly stories and rumours we seem to have fallen prey to over the last few days,' she continued, raising her eyebrows in a way you could totally tell meant 'bonkeroonie lies', 'Mr Falconer has kindly agreed to stay on and answer students' questions in the main hall after lunch. Your form teachers will take afternoon registration as usual but, in the meantime, I suggest you think about what you'd like to ask Mr Falconer.'

She swept out of the room with Jim Falconer (who clearly wasn't Time Lord in disguise) hot on her clacking heels.

'Blimey,' said Abs.

'You know what this means?' I said.

'Yep. First period maths is cancelled,' Soph nodded.

I leant back in my chair, grinning. This film thing was just getting better and better!

'Of course, some of us have already met him,' I heard a voice saying behind me.

'Was that in your private coaching lesson?' said another voice.

I kept completely still in my leaning-back position. It was seriously uncomfortable, but I'm always prepared to suffer for nosiness.

'Yep. Time Lord introduced me as his star pupil,' said the first voice. Amanda Hawkins. What joy. 'He had to cut our session short for today because he had important stuff to discuss with Jim.'

'Like what?' said someone else. Considering Amanda wasn't calling them names, insulting their parents or trying to nick their lunch money, I guessed the other two voices belonged to her vile-issimo cronies, Lara Neils and Keira Roberts.

'Well,' said Amanda, 'I couldn't hang around for long, but I did hear them talking about who's going to be in the film. As well as Estelle Mayor there's going to be another girl and two boys.'

I could feel my celeb radar springing into action. *Four* film stars actually here in our school for, like, the entire summer! I sooo had to ace the audition and become an extra!

'Did he say who they were?' asked Lara. Or maybe Keira.

'Oh, yeah,' said Amanda, and I heard a chair scraping. 'Come on, I feel like a bit of fresh air. I'll tell you outside.'

I leaned back as far as I could, straining harder than ever to hear, in case Amanda said anything else as they walked out. A second later, I was flat on my back with my legs in the air, probably showing my knickers to half the canteen.

'Did you see that?' I said, as Abs and Soph helped me out of my tipped-over chair.

'Yeah,' said Soph. 'Your knickers sooo don't match your uniform.'

'Not *that*,' I said, still feeling a bit red in the face. 'Amanda.'

'Hmmm,' said Abs, looking a bit fidgety.

'D'you think they saw me ear-wigging?' I said.

'Totally,' said Abs.

But I never say never when it comes to fishing for celeb gossip. No, sireee! There was something juicy to be uncovered here, and I just had to find out what.